TOM McCAUGHREN is on
writers of books for young pe
books have won awards and h
other languages.

His first books for young people were the *The Legend of the Golden Key, The Legend of the Phantom Highwayman* and *The Legend of the Corrib King.* These proved so popular that they have now been published in longer format with new illustrations. The legend series was followed by *The Children of the Forge* and *The Silent Sea,* all of them winners for readers in the 9-14 age group.

In 1989, his novel for teenagers, *Rainbows of the Moon,* was published by Anvil Books, parent company of The Children's Press. It was short-listed for the Irish Book Awards in 1990 and the following year saw arrangements for its translation, into French.

His fox books, *Run with the Wind, Run to Earth,* and *Run Swift, Run Free,* published by Wolfhound Press, have been translated into Swedish, German, and Japanese. They have also won the Reading Association of Ireland Book Award, the Irish Book Awards Medal, the Irish Children's Book Trust Bisto Book of the Decade Award and the White Raven's Selection of the International Youth Library in Munich.

A fourth book in this series, *Run to the Ark,* was published in 1991.

A journalist, Tom is RTE's Security Correspondent. He is married and has four daughters.

Tom McCaughren

The Legend of the Phantom Highwayman

Illustrated by Terry Myler

THE CHILDREN'S PRESS

To
William Rodgers

First published 1983 by
The Children's Press
45 Palmerston Road, Dublin 6.

This enlarged edition 1991

ISBN 0 947962 58 1

Typeset by Computertype Limited
Printed by Billing & Sons

This book is financially assisted by
The Arts Council/An Chomhairle Ealaíon, Ireland.

CONTENTS

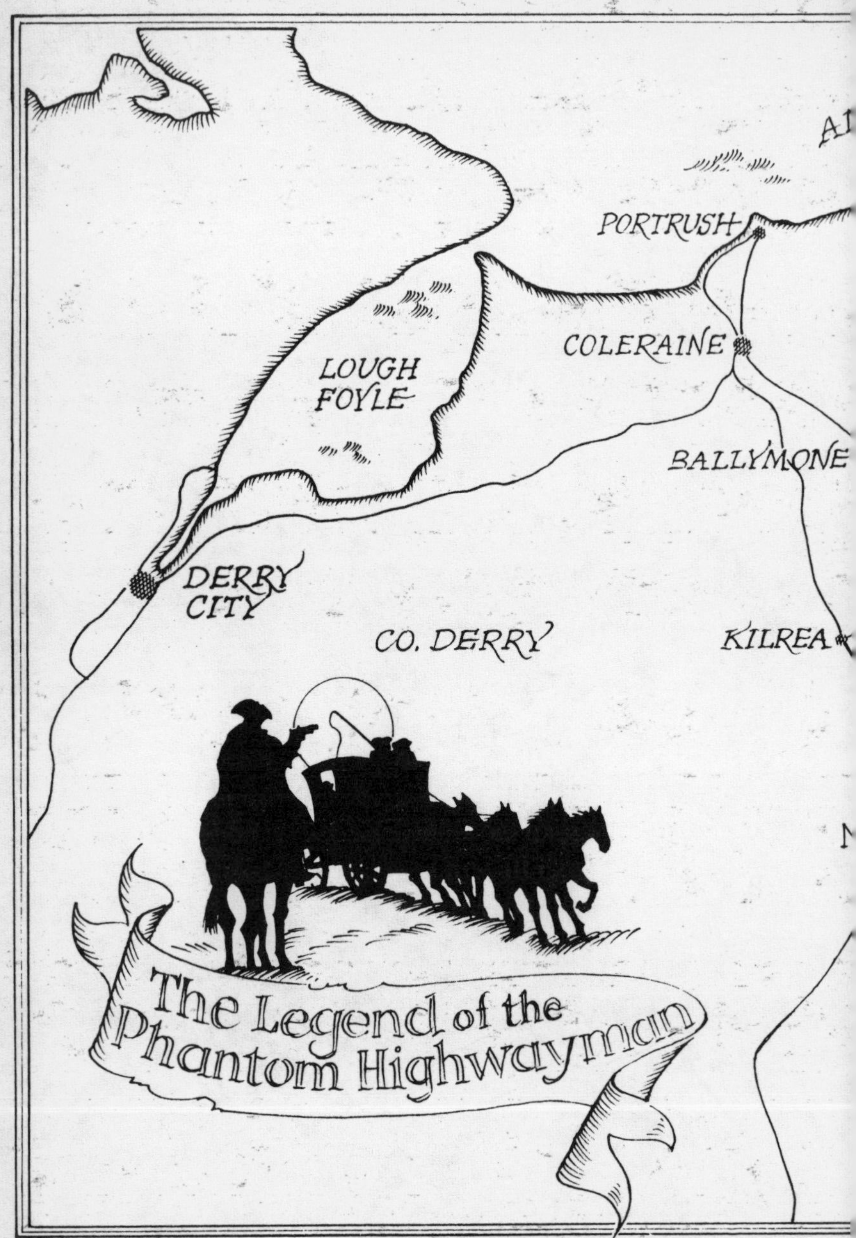
PORTRUSH
COLERAINE
LOUGH FOYLE
BALLYMONE
DERRY CITY
CO. DERRY
KILREA
The Legend of the Phantom Highwayman

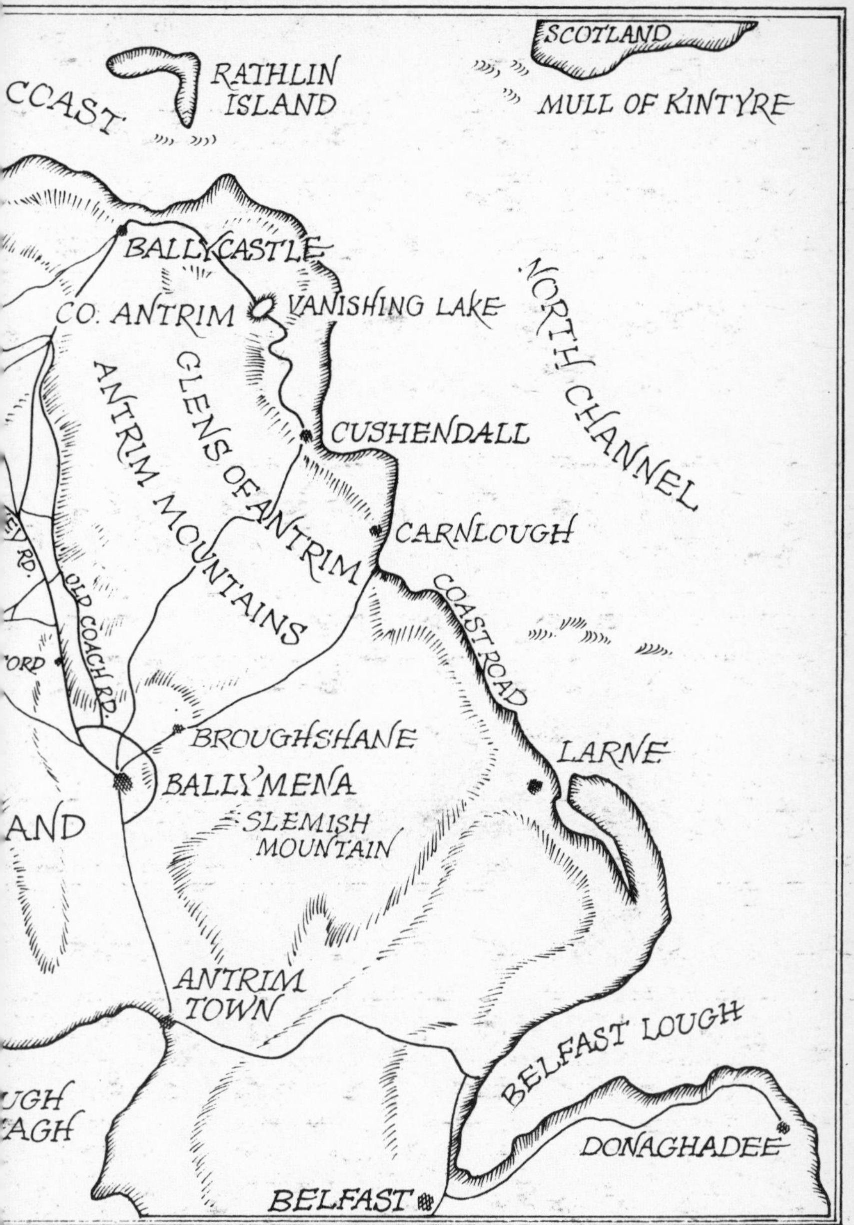
SCOTLAND
RATHLIN
ISLAND
MULL OF KINTYRE
COAST
BALLYCASTLE
VANISHING LAKE
CO. ANTRIM
NORTH CHANNEL
GLENS OF ANTRIM
ANTRIM MOUNTAINS
CUSHENDALL
CARNLOUGH
COAST ROAD
OLD COACH RD.
RD.
ORD
BROUGHSHANE
LARNE
BALLYMENA
AND
SLEMISH
MOUNTAIN
ANTRIM
TOWN
BELFAST LOUGH
UGH
AGH
DONAGHADEE
BELFAST

INTRODUCTION

During the eighteenth century and early part of the last century, when the stage coach services were spreading throughout Ireland, highwaymen were a serious problem. Sometimes operating in groups, sometimes alone, they would appear on lonely country roads to hold up coaches at pistol-point and rob the passengers.

Posters were put up offering rewards for information leading to the capture of the highwaymen, and various steps were taken to protect passengers. Soldiers on horseback escorted coaches through remote mountain areas and other places where highwaymen were likely to strike. At first the mail coaches carried one armed guard, but by the turn of the century they had started to carry two. In 1808, an inducement held out to passengers on the Dublin-Cork route was that a newly-acquired coach was copper-lined and therefore bullet-proof!

In spite of such precautions, some travellers continued to find themselves looking into the pistols of highwaymen demanding, 'Your money or your life'. In 1827, for example, a £50 reward was offered for information about the person or persons who had attacked the Dublin to Cork mail coach and fired a shot, the contents of which, to quote the poster, 'passed through the hat of one of the passengers.'

The robbing of travellers, of course, didn't begin with the stage coaches. Many a luckless person was waylaid and robbed in the days when the only way to get around was by foot or on horseback. Indeed, there was a time when it was usual for people intending to go on a journey to make their will, in case they might meet an untimely end at the hands of a robber.

Some of the more notable highwaymen were people who had fought for one lost cause or another, while some had been dispossessed of their lands. Inevitably, a number have been portrayed as Robin Hood characters who robbed the rich to help the poor. Many others, it must be said, had no such pretensions, and whether they were local heroes or common criminals, highwaymen were hunted relentlessly by the authorities, and most of them met the same fate - death by hanging.

Since this book was first published in somewhat shorter form in 1983, many young readers have asked me if Hugh Rua, the legendary figure in the story, was a real highwayman. Well, all I can say is, he could have been! However, all the other highwaymen mentioned did exist.

Thomas Archer, for example, was a fugitive from the 1798 Rebellion. For two years his bands of 'brigands' as they were called, roamed the Ballymena area of Co. Antrim where this book begins.

There's a story in *Old Ballymena*, a collection of articles originally published in the local *Observer* newspaper in 1857, that shortly before Archer's capture, he had murdered a loyalist farmer with whom he had had a violent row 'on the public road'.

Some years ago I heard a similar story from a neighbour of mine in Ballymena, Mr. William Rodgers, on whom the character, Mr. Stockman in this book is based.

Mr. Rodgers, who was in his eighties at the time, said his grandfather told him he knew Archer. He also told him how a local farmer had recognized the highwayman at Kilrea Fair. The farmer threatened to tell the Redcoats, as the British soldiers were known, and that night Archer arrived at the man's home where he shot and killed him.

While the name of the farmer given in the two accounts is different, they seem to relate to the same incident, and Mr. Rodger's account, which he confirmed to me shortly before he died, suggests a motive for the murder.

A coach similar to the *Londonderry Mail*, which features in this book, may be seen in the Ulster Folk and Transport Museum at Cultra, Holywood, Co. Down, and a visit to the museum is recommended.

My interest in stage coaches, and the idea for this story, go back to my boyhood days in Ballymena. My father, who worked for Ballymena Borough Council, told me about the coaches and how, on their journeys from Belfast to Derry, they would have come up through Coach Entry, where the council stabled some of its horses, and then on to the Old Coach Road near our home.

Coach Entry, incidentally, is off Castle Street where Archer was born, and opposite a large Norman mound called the Moat, where he was hanged.

It was when I was working as a young reporter in Ballymena that I first came across the practice of poteen-making, which also features in the *Highwayman*. Poteen is a kind of whiskey, it's home-made and it's illegal as the law only allows whiskey to be made in licensed distilleries. I remember covering a number of prosecutions against poteen-makers when I travelled to the Glens of Antrim with my friend, solicitor Jack McCann, to attend hearings of the local court. Later, as I pursued my journalistic career in other parts of the country I found that poteen-making wasn't confined to Co. Antrim!

As a boy I also visited the glens, gazing in wonder at the sheer beauty of what the glaciers had left behind. Sometimes I would be going with my parents or other members of my family to the 'shore' as the seaside there is called. On other occasions I might be lucky enough to be accompanying Mr. Rodgers when he was delivering confectionery to shops in the glens. The delights of such a journey in a van full of sweets and chocolate are obvious, and there was great competition to see who would be allowed to go with him. As a result, he was never short of willing hands when it came to loading his van from the store room on his farm or collecting supplies from Giffin's Sweet Factory on the Waveney Road in Ballymena. I hope young readers will enjoy my account of the 'sweet run' and the adventure it leads them to in what I have called, *The Legend of the Phantom Highwayman.*

Tom McCaughren
1991

1. HEARING THINGS

From the darkness of his bedroom, Tapser listened to the babble of voices in the kitchen. He had gone to bed early as he was getting a lift to the glen with Mr. Stockman next day, and was lying wondering what his visit was going to be like. He loved those seemingly rare occasions when Mr. Stockman took the day off from farming to deliver sweets to small shops along the mountains and in the glen. The sweet run they all called it, and a sweet run it was in every sense of the word. He was also looking forward to seeing his cousin Cowlick again. They always had great fun together. Last year, when Cowlick had visited him, they had helped to solve the mystery of *The Legend of the Golden Key*. That was a great adventure, and he wondered if they would find anything exciting to do in the glen. Suddenly, as he lay and thought about these things, he became aware of what one of the neighbours was saying . . .

'That may well be, but the glensfolk say there's something funny going on.'

'How do you mean?' asked Mr. Stockman.

'Ah, wouldn't you know, the quare stuff of course.'

'Not to mention Hugh Rua,' said another. 'They say he's been seen again.'

'Aye,' laughed Tapser's father, 'it wouldn't do if you ran into the phantom highwayman.'

'Och now,' said Mr. Stockman, ' I never met a man yet that saw a phantom.'

'If there's no such thing,' said the second man, 'what does the ballad mean? How does it go now?'

Tapser then heard him singing:

'Stand and deliver,' said Hugh Rua
'Stand and deliver, do or die . . .'
He stole a coach-and-four
So they hung him on the moor.
But they say his spirit still rides in the glen . . .

'There you are,' said Tapser's father. 'Somebody must have seen him.'

'Well, if anyone asks me to stand and deliver,' joked Mr. Stockman, 'all he'll get is a delivery of sweets.'

They all laughed at that, and Tapser sat up and rubbed his eyes. He couldn't believe his ears. He wanted to hear more but knew if he went into the kitchen they would probably change the subject, so he slipped out of bed and listened at the door.

'If anyone stops you, it's more likely to be the police,' said the first man.

'What for?' asked Mr. Stockman.

'Didn't I tell you, to see who's smuggling the quare stuff.'

Tapser was dying to hear more, but the men went on to talk about the barley crop and the price it would fetch. He got back into bed and snuggled under the clothes. Thoughts of highwaymen and smugglers filled his mind. What did they mean by 'the quare stuff' he wondered? And what was all this about a phantom highwayman? Was there really something going on in the glen, or was this just another of their ghost stories? The trouble was he never really knew when they were serious.

There was great excitement next morning as last-minute preparations were made for the journey. Tapser's mother was fussing around wondering if there was anything they had forgotten to pack. Even his collie, Prince, was excited, almost as if he knew what was happening. Then Mr. Stockman called to say he was about to load the van and would Tapser give him a hand. Tapser, of course, was only too delighted.

The sweet store was like an Aladdin's cave, and Tapser and his friends always felt privileged any time they were allowed into it. Not because they got any sweets there — it wasn't until they were on their way to the glen that they got those. It was simply the smell of the store, a sweet musty odour that appealed to their nostrils and to their imaginations so much. It was a smell like honeysuckle, a smell that was the essence of bulls' eyes, and toffees, and sticks of pink rock, and chocolate and lollypops, and all the other sweet things they wanted to buy in the shops but could seldom afford. It was a smell that held the magic of promise .

'Now, Tapser,' said Mr. Stockman, nodding to the deep shelves along one wall. 'We'll take the jars first, and be careful you don't drop them.'

He handed down a big glass jar of barley sugar, and Tapser, hugging it as he would a baby in case he might drop it and ruin the trip, gingerly stepped around the tea chests and boxes that were piled about the store, and made his way out to the van.

Soon the van was loaded with a mouth-watering selection of all that was in the store, including jars of butter-scotch, acid drops and clove rock, not to mention cardboard boxes, the contents of which could only be imagined. Tapser took his place in the front passenger seat, Prince hopped in and sat between his legs, and, with his mother shouting after him not to forget to do this and not to forget to do that, the blue van rounded the pillars at the foot of the lane, and headed up the hill towards the Old Coach Road.

Tapser, of course, could hardly contain his curiosity about the phantom highwayman. He didn't want to ask straight out and let Mr. Stockman know he had been listening to them the night before, but as they turned into the Old Coach Road, he got an idea.

'Why do they call this the Old Coach Road?' he asked.

'Because that's exactly what it is,' explained Mr. Stockman. 'In olden days this was the main road from Belfast to Ballymena, Ballymoney and on to Derry. Of course it wasn't a good tarmacadam road like it is now. There were no motorcars and no railways, and the only way of getting from one place to another, unless you walked or had a horse, was by stage coach.'

'But I thought they only had stage coaches in the Wild West,' said Tapser.

Mr. Stockman shook his head and watched the road in front of him. 'Not at all. Sure they had coaches in this part of the world long before they had them in America.'

'But why did they call them stage coaches?' asked Tapser.

'Because they did the journey in stages, I suppose. You can just imagine what some of the roads were like in the days before Mr. McAdam thought of a way of making better ones'.

'Who was Mr. McAdam?'

'John Loudon McAdam. He was a Scottish engineer who came up with the idea of giving the roads a harder, smoother surface. That's why it's called tarmacadam. Before that it was rough going, and as well as picking up passengers, the coachman had to stop here and there to feed and water the horses or get a fresh team.'

Tapser could just imagine it, for in the sweet store he had often admired a picture in which the driver of a cart had stopped at the river in Ballymena to allow his horse to have a drink. In the background was the old spinning mill. Mr. Rodgers had told him that in years gone by, when the farmers of the area had grown flax for making linen, the picture had been an advertisement for the Braidwater Spinning Company.

As they passed under the motorway and drove towards the Antrim mountains, Mr. Stockman continued, 'Of course, the highways the stage coaches used are only the by-roads of today.'

'Why did they call them highways?' asked Tapser.

'Oh, I don't know . . . probably because they were always higher than the fields.'

'And is that where the highwaymen got their name?'

'That's right — from robbing coaches on the King's highway.'

'Boy, they must have been exciting times.'

'Aye, and dangerous.'

'You mean, because of the highwaymen?'

Mr. Stockman nodded. 'There was a famous highwayman here in the Ballymena area, you know.'

Tapser looked at him to see if he was serious.

'There was. His name was Thomas Archer. He was a fugitive from the 1798 Rebellion.'

The road to the village of Broughshane branched off to the right, and Mr. Stockman continued, 'The United Irishmen had marched on Ballymena from Broughshane. They laid siege to the Town Hall, or the Market House as it was called then, and after a battle, set fire to it. Some of the defenders, a small group of yeomen and loyalists, were killed during the battle or done to death afterwards.'

Mr. Stockman changed gear as they went uphill. 'However, the rebel victory was short-lived. When the rising was defeated up in Antrim town, the troops arrived in Ballymena. The rebels were forced to retreat and some of them were hanged on top of the Moat for all to see.'

Tapser was trying to imagine the scene on top of the Norman fort they called the Moat — a large mound which was now a children's playground — when Mr. Stockman added, 'Then they cut off their heads and stuck them on pitchforks on the parapet of the Market House as a warning to others never to do the like again.'

Tapser shivered at the thought.

'The last man to be executed,' continued Mr. Stockman, 'was Archer, the outlaw. When the rebellion broke out, he deserted from the Antrim militia and joined the rebels. Afterwards he went on the run and became known as the Brigand of Ballymena.'

'Would you call him a highwayman then?' asked Tapser.

'Well, he certainly carried out a lot of robberies, and he was said to be very daring. Sometimes he would disguise himself as a woman, and with his blunderbuss hidden under his cloak, visit his parents up in Castle Street.'

'What's a blunderbuss?' asked Tapser.

'It was like a single-barrelled shot-gun, only shorter, and it widened out at the end like a trumpet. Anyway, as I was saying, he was supposed to be very daring. But he was also a very violent man and him and his gang murdered a loyalist farmer up near Glarryford. Soon after that he was captured and hanged on the Moat like the others.'

'Did they cut off his head too?'

'I don't know. But like many another highwaymen his body was put in irons and left hanging there until it was only a skeleton.'

'What other highwaymen?' asked Tapser, hoping Mr. Stockman would tell him about Hugh Rua.

'Well, there was Captain Brennan on the Moor as he was known, down in Tipperary. The same thing happened to him.'

They were well on their way now.

'And what about the glens?' asked Tapser. 'Did they have a highwayman?'

Mr. Stockman smiled and nodded. 'Of course they did — and still have, by all accounts. His name is Hugh Rua.'

'What do you mean "still have"? Sure highwaymen lived hundreds of years ago. You're after saying so yourself.'

'I know that. But Hugh Rua still rides in the glen – or so they say.'

Tapser looked at him. 'You don't really believe that, do you? I mean, how could he?'

Mr. Stockman was still smiling to himself. When he wasn't busy on the farm he loved a bit of fun, and enjoyed the sweet run just as much as any of the young people who went with him. 'Well ... the glens have a lot of secrets you know. So have the people.'

'And what did you say his name was?'

'Hugh Rua. He had red hair, just like yourself. So he was known as Hugh Rua, or Red Hugh. Probably Hugh of the Red Beard.'

'That's a funny sort of name.'

'Not really. Some highwaymen were known by their own names, like Archer. Or the three O'Haughan brothers, who were highwaymen here in Antrim long before Archer's time. But sometimes they were given romantic names, like Sean Mullen of Derry. He was known as Sean Crosagh, the outlaw. Then there was Cathal Mór of South Armagh — Big Charley. And Cahir na gCapall, Charles of the Horses, in Laois. He was a horse thief.'

'You seem to know an awful lot about highwaymen,' said Tapser.

'That's because I've been reading about them.'

'Were you trying to find out more about Hugh Rua?'

Mr. Stockman glanced over at him. 'Aren't you very curious now?'

'But did you?' asked Tapser.

'Did I what?'

'Did you find out anything more about Hugh Rua?'

'Not a whole lot,' Mr. Stockman admitted. 'But don't worry. You'll find out plenty about him down in the glen. He's regarded as a hero there.'

'How come,' asked Tapser.

'Well, legend has it that when the glensfolk were very poor, he rode up out of the glen to rob the rich. A sort of Robin Hood. Then he overdid it and stole a coach, so he ended up on the gallows like Archer.'

'You mean, they hanged him?'

'Aye. They stood for no nonsense in them days. For some crimes, even small ones, it was transportation to Australia. For murder and highway robbery, it was the gallows. But Hugh Rua's legend is very much alive in the glen. In fact, there's been a lot of talk of him recently. You see, some people say they've seen him on the High Road in the dead of night. Or if it wasn't him, it was his ghost.'

Tapser was bursting with questions now and Mr. Stockman judged it was time for a breathing space, so he promptly told him to reach into the back and get a handful of sweets.

The squat featureless shape of Slemish Mountain loomed large on their right, and as the blue van made its way through the countryside, Mr. Stockman turned his attention to the crops. A small man with wispy grey hair, his face was tinged with red from a lifetime spent in the open.

It was a good year, he was thinking, and the barley was standing well — no lodging from heavy rain and high winds as so often happened. Now as he relaxed and thought about the harvest, he began to whistle to himself.

'What's that?' asked Tapser, curious to know what the tune was as it had a nice lilt to it.

Mr. Stockman smiled and gave him a few bars of the song:

Gather up the pots and the oul' tin can
The mash, the corn, the barley and the bran
Run like the divil from the Excise man
Keep the smoke from rising Barney . . .

'That's a funny song,' said Tapser. 'What's it about?'

Mr. Stockman turned his head slightly and winked. 'The quare stuff.'

Tapser's ears pricked up immediately. That's what they had been talking about the night before — the quare stuff. But what was it?

Seeing he was puzzled, Mr. Stockman told him, 'The quare stuff — poteen.'

'What's that?'

'Poteen,' said Mr. Stockman. 'Well, I suppose you could say it's home-made whiskey. It's the drink of mountain folk — glensfolk too when they can smuggle down a bottle.'

Slemish, which had seemed to keep pace with them for a while, was now beginning to slip away behind them.

'But why do they have to smuggle it?' asked Tapser.

'Because it's against the law to make it. That's why the song says, *Run like the divil from the Excise man.* The

Excise men are the Customs and they control that sort of thing.'

'But why are people not allowed to make it?'

'Because you have to have a licence to make whiskey and then you have to pay so much money or taxes to the Government. The poteen-makers do it on the quiet, and, apart from the fact that they don't pay tax, there's nobody to check how good or bad it is. And if you get bad stuff it could damage your insides. Maybe even drive you round the bend.'

'And why do you call it the quare stuff?'

'Well, I suppose because it's made in queer circumstances and it can have a queer effect on you. They also call it mountain dew, because unlike whiskey it's as clear as the dew on the grass. Or 'wee still' because it's made in small stills. In America they call it moonshine. But it's the same thing. They say a drop of it can cure you; too much can kill you.'

'You mentioned barley in the song. What's that got to do with poteen?'

'Man dear,' said Mr. Stockman, using one of his favourite phrases of affection, 'isn't that what they make it with.'

'Barley? I thought that was used for making flour.'

'Not at all,' said Mr. Stockman, at a loss to understand how Tapser could have spent so many summers on his farm and not know what barley was used for. 'Flour is made from wheat. Barley is used for making feeding-stuff for livestock or for making whiskey. And, as I say, they also use it to make a wee drop of poteen when the police aren't looking.'

Who 'they' were, Tapser couldn't imagine, but he hoped it was something he might find out during his visit.

They were now approaching the mountains that would lead them to the glen and at a remote crossroads they stopped at a small shop to deliver sweets. Before leaving, Mr. Stockman struck up a conversation with a local man and was pleased to learn that a corncrake had been heard in the area in spite of the fact that they had almost been wiped out by the continual cutting of grass for silage. Larks, which were suffering the same fate, had also been seen farther up the hill, he was told.

The man was telling no lie, for when a short time later they stopped at the top of the glen and got out to admire the view, they could hear the unmistakeable song of a

lark as it fluttered high in the sky. Here and there the sides of the glen were aglow with the red berries of the rowan tree or mountain ash. Lower down, golden fields of barley formed a patchwork quilt with various shades of green. And beyond lay the blue expanse of the sea.

Tapser shaded his eyes with his hand and asked, 'Is that Rathlin Island?'

Mr. Stockman shaded his eyes too and told him, 'No, that's Scotland. Rathlin's farther up the coast, near Ballycastle.'

Tapser tried to take it all in, and when he could strain his eyes no farther than the hazy blue outline on the horizon, he switched his gaze back in towards the shore. Fishermen in small boats were tending to their lobster pots and nets. In the little harbour, a ship was unloading cargo.

Mr. Stockman pointed to a building that rose up out of the scrub on the left side of the glen. It was white and glistened brightly in the sun.

'That's the Castle Spa Hotel down on the Low Road.'

'What's a spa?' asked Tapser.

'A spring well,' said Mr. Stockman. 'The one there is supposed to have been blessed by St. Patrick, and they say the water has great healing power. As a slave, Patrick herded swine on the slopes of Slemish, you know. And over there on the right, beside the High Road, you'll find a memorial to Hugh Rua. That's where they hanged him.'

As the van free-wheeled its way down into the glen, Tapser couldn't help wondering about Hugh Rua and what Mr. Stockman had said about the people of the glen. Did they really have a lot of secrets? And was the Legend of the Phantom Highwayman one of them?

2 THE SPIRIT OF THE GLEN

When the van pulled into the yard, Cowlick's mother and father gave Mr. Stockman and Tapser a hearty welcome. A few minutes later Cowlick rushed around the end of the house to greet them too. He was followed by the farm's two sheepdogs which pranced around, resenting Prince, but finally accepting the bigger male collie with a submissive lowering of their tails.

It was dinner time, and the two visitors were ushered into the kitchen. It was a typical farmhouse, big and warm and smelling of boiled potatoes and freshly baked soda bread. Cowlick's mother, a plump homely woman, had already laid the table, and when they had taken their places she filled their plates with lavish helpings of bacon and cabbage.

Unlike Mr. Stockman, Cowlick's father was a big burly man. He had a ruddy complexion, sparse sandy hair and a hearty laugh, and as they peeled their potatoes he told

Mr. Stockman he was waiting for the combine harvester to arrive in the morning.'

Just then, Cowlick's sisters, Roisin and Rachel, burst in and dumped a bucket beside the kitchen sink. They had been picking blackberries up the side of the glen and had run all the way down. The berries were for making jam but, as their mother observed, it was plain to see they had been eating them too. As a result they had to contain their excitement until they rushed upstairs and gave their hands and faces a quick wash.

When the dinner was over, the two men went off to look at some livestock in the back yard, and Cowlick and his sisters showed Tapser where he would be sleeping. An old rambling farmhouse, it had a big unused sitting-room with old-fashioned pictures of lone stags in mountain settings, other smaller rooms here and there, narrow corridors, steep stairs, and what seemed a lot of bedrooms.

Tapser was delighted to learn he wouldn't be sleeping on his own, but would be sharing a room with Cowlick. He had just brought up his case when they were told Mr. Stockman was leaving, so they all rushed down to say good-bye.

Mr. Stockman told them he would be going to the Lammas Fair at Ballycastle the following Monday and would call and collect Tapser on his way home. He gave each of them a handful of sweets and with a wave left to make the rest of his deliveries.

When the blue van had disappeared from their view, the others asked Tapser what he would like to do. Of course, after the drive with Mr. Stockman, the only things he had in mind were poteen-makers and Hugh Rua. Poteen-makers they'd never find, his cousins told him, but if he wanted to find out more about Hugh Rua, why not? So they immediately set off for the High Road and the site of the memorial to the highwayman.

Prince explored a variety of scents as they climbed up through the thick scrub on the side of the glen. Here and there a small stream cascaded over the edge and fell in a long thin waterfall. Currents of air carried a fine spray back up like a wisp of smoke, and plucked at the girls' long blonde hair when they reached the top.

Tapser found that the High Road ran between the edge of the glen and a bog, curling out of the mountains and disappearing down to the sea. Just beside it, on a prominent patch of rocky ground overlooking the glen, was the memorial to Hugh Rua.

The memorial was about three feet high and in the form of a bronze horse and rider. The horse was rearing up and its rider, masked and with a flowing cape, held a blunderbuss in his right hand. Tapser ran his fingers over the plaque on the granite base, and read the inscription aloud:

ERECTED TO THE MEMORY OF HUGH RUA
HIGHWAYMAN AND FRIEND OF THE GLEN.
CAPTURED BY THE KING'S DRAGOONS,
AND HANGED ON THIS SPOT
IN THE YEAR OF OUR LORD, 1813.

'And look,' said Tapser. 'Down here it says,

"HIS SPIRIT STILL RIDES IN THE GLEN."

That's from the ballad, isn't it? What does it mean? His ghost?'

'Well, there has been talk about that sort of thing recently,' said Roisin, flicking away hair that had blown across her face. 'But there's more to it than that.'

'That's right,' said Cowlick. 'But you'd need to know the people down here to understand what they mean.'

'For goodness sake,' Rachel chipped in impatiently, 'there's no mystery about it. The people here in the glen, well, they're different. They're very independent, and in the days of Hugh Rua they were very poor and they felt they were being neglected. The stage coaches were going into other areas, but not the glen as the roads were too bad.'

'That's right,' said Roisin, taking up the story. 'The people felt that if they had proper roads the stage coaches would come through, it would open up the glen and they would be more prosperous.'

'So one day,' continued Rachel, 'Hugh Rua, who had often ridden up out of the glen to rob the coach from Belfast, actually stole a coach and four horses on their way to Derry and brought them to the glen.'

'Just to draw attention to the problem,' explained Cowlick, who had been nodding in agreement.

'But then they caught him,' said Roisin, 'and hanged him for highway robbery up here in full view of the whole glen so that everyone would see it and learn their lesson.'

'So now you know,' said Cowlick, 'why people here consider Hugh Rua a sort of hero, even if he was a highwayman.'

As Tapser thought about what they had said and looked at the bronze horse and rider, he could visualize it coming to life at night to haunt the High Road. Then he read the last line on the plaque:

ERECTED BY THE PEOPLE OF THE GLEN
WITH THE GENEROUS ASSISTANCE OF
THE CASTLE SPA

'How come?' he asked.

'Max put up the money for it — to mark Hugh Rua's one hundred and seventieth anniversary,' Roisin told him.

'Max van Weshal,' explained Cowlick, and nodding towards the big white building on the far side of the glen added, 'He owns the Castle Spa.'

'Apart from giving money towards the memorial,' said Tapser, 'I don't suppose he'd know any more about Hugh Rua than you do?'

'Hardly,' said Cowlick. 'He probably only contributed to the memorial to keep in with the local people. There was a lot of resentment when he came here and bought the Castle Spa.'

'You know what country people are like,' explained Roisin. 'They won't buy something themselves but they don't want anyone else to buy it, especially a foreigner. It's the same everywhere, that's what mammy says anyway.'

'Look,' cried Rachel, pointing down at the farmhouse. 'There's Peppi. Come on.'

'Who's Peppi? ' Tapser asked Cowlick as they followed at a trot.

'He's the eggman. Well, he's more than an eggman really. He's a peddlar. That's his caravan pulling into the yard. He buys eggs and sells almost everything and he sharpens almost anything on a contraption he has at the back. He's great fun.'

Tapser could see that Peppi was very popular, as there was a great competition to see who could get down to the yard first. The girls had got a head start and were there before them.

'Where did he get a name like Peppi?' asked Tapser.

'Oh, from the girls,' replied Cowlick, as if to say,

wouldn't you know. ' It comes from the first letters of the sign on his caravan.'

When they rounded the corner of the house, Tapser saw what he meant. Peppi's caravan was parked in the yard. Drawn by a single brown horse, it was a high, rectangular affair, with four red-spoked wheels. It had a covering of faded green canvas, and an almost flat top that stuck out in front to give shelter to the driver. Painted on the side was the sign:

PANDORA & CO.
EGGS COLLECTED
POTS AND
PANS FOR SALE
IN PART EXCHANGE FOR CASH

There was a small chimney sticking up through the roof at the front, and towards the back, which was open, hung a variety of pots and pans, hurricane lamps, saws and coils of wire, as well as some antique fire-irons and other brasses.

Peppi, having danced around with the girls and given them an affectionate hug, hopped up into the back of the caravan and came back out with a particular type of thread they had asked him to get. It was a thread they needed for school, and their mother hadn't been able to get it for them.

Cowlick introduced Tapser. 'Just call me Peppi,' he said with a laugh. 'Everyone else does.'

Peppi was indeed a very likeable person, as Cowlick had suggested. He was quite a young man, with black wavy hair and a happy face. He smoked a curly pipe and wore woollen gloves cut off at the fingers.

Tapser thought he looked the type of young man who,

EGGS

rather than accept unemployment in the town, had struck out on his own and was depending on goodwill and sheer energy to make a living. For there he was now, peddling the contraption at the back of the caravan and sharpening a variety of kitchen knives that the girls had fetched from the house. Then he was busily storing eggs safely into the caravan and counting out the money to their mother.

'What do you make of him?' asked Cowlick as Peppi and his father exchanged a few words.

'Seems a nice person,' said Tapser. 'Why?'

'We all like him. But the girls think it's suspicious the why he always wears those woollen gloves. I think it's just because of all the work he does with his hands. But the girls think there is some other reason.'

As they looked at the woollen gloves again, Cowlick's father was saying, 'Any chance of a drop of poteen in there?', nodding to the caravan.

'Ah, you never know,' laughed Peppi. Then, in a somewhat confidential tone, 'I hear there's a lot of it coming down from the mountains these days, and neither the police nor the Army can stop it getting out.'

'Do you tell me now,' said Cowlick's father. 'But sure, what's new about that? Aren't they for ever making it up there. The Widow Mulqueen has always a few bottles coming along. They don't call her the Queen of the Mountain Dew for nothing you know.'

'True, true,' said Peppi, sucking his pipe. 'But the word is someone is in it in a big way now, and the police are out to get them. It's not just a question of the wee still any more, but a big still.'

Everyone pricked up their ears at the mention of the poteen-makers.

'And that's not all,' continued Peppi. 'I hear the ghost

of Hugh Rua was seen on the High Road again last night.'

'Ah, would you go on out of that,' laughed the farmer, waving him away as if to say he had more important things to do than listen to talk like that. 'Anyway, what's that got to do with it?'

'Oh you may laugh if you like,' said Peppi, serious all of a sudden. 'But the way I hear it, when Hugh Rua appears it's a sure sign there's a shipment of the quare stuff on the way.'

The combine harvester arrived next morning, but no sooner had it started to cut the barley than a mechanical fault developed, and Tapser and his cousins watched as two men worked to get it going again. Another man, in a white coat, was telling them what to do.

'The one in the white supervising them is Max van Weshal,' said Cowlick.

'What's he doing here?' asked Tapser. 'I thought you said he owned the Castle Spa?'

'He does,' Rachel told him. 'But he does a lot more besides. He's an engineer, and when any of the heavy machinery breaks down he and his men come and fix it. '

'I thought you said people resented him?'

'Some do,' said Roisin. 'That's because he has great ideas and they're jealous.'

'What sort of ideas?'

'Well, for a start,' Cowlick told him, 'he came up with the idea of closing down the hotel and selling water from the spa instead.'

'Selling water? How can you sell water?'

'I don't know, but he exports it. They say he even built his own bottling plant.'

'And then there are the lobsters,' said Rachel. 'He's got bigger boats and goes out farther and catches more than anyone else.'

'That's why people resent him,' said Roisin. 'He does everything so scientifically.'

Tapser could well believe it, for even though Max was quite young, his short-cropped fair hair and rimless glasses gave the impression of a man who was both brainy and efficient. 'And the other two?'

'They're his fixers,' said Cowlick. 'I don't know their real names, but they're foreigners too.'

'They also work on the lobster boats,' said Roisin, 'so we call the big one with the seaman's cap Whaler.'

Tapser smiled. He could see the name was very apt, for the man was very big and heavy. Unlike the other, an excitable little man with sallow skin and black greasy hair.

Rachel giggled. 'We call the wee one Scamp, because he's always scampering around doing what Max tells him.'

'You wouldn't think anyone as serious as Max would have a sense of humour,' Roisin went on. 'But he has. You should see the sign he has over the shops at the Castle Spa.'

'It's a funny sense of humour if you ask me,' remarked Rachel.

'He can sing a song too when he's in the mood,' said Cowlick. 'His party piece is the *Ballad of Hugh Rua*. Come on, I'll introduce you.'

With a slight bow of his head, Max shook hands with Tapser and in a faintly foreign accent told him, 'Perhaps I will see you at the Castle Spa sometime.' Then he added, 'When I'm not busy, of course.'

Tapser didn't quite know what to make of Max.

Nevertheless, he was every bit as efficient as the others had said, and it wasn't long before he and his men had the combine harvester going again. Soon the giant machine was swallowing up great swards of barley and spewing the golden grain into big high-sided trailers and lorries.

Living as he did some distance from the sea, Tapser wanted to go to the beach, so they hitched a lift into town with the first load of barley.

A short time later as they walked along the sand, they amused themselves by throwing sticks into the sea for Prince to retrieve. The collie was obviously delighted to be at the seaside too. He barked and barked as each stick was thrown and plunged in after it.

Searching around for another stick, Tapser picked up a bottle that had floated in on the tide.

'What is it?' asked Cowlick.

'A bottle of spa water,' said Tapser, reading the label. 'Just what we need. I'm parched.' Unscrewing the cap, he put the bottle to his lips. 'Ughhh . . .' he spluttered, spitting it out. 'It's not water at all.'

'You're right,' said Cowlick, sniffing the bottle. 'It's not. It's poteen!'

His sisters also sniffed the bottle and confirmed that that was what it was.

'Maybe Peppi was right then,' Tapser exclaimed. 'Maybe the smugglers are on the move again!'

3 THE RAID

The sun was high in the sky now and it was warm. The four sat down at the foot of the rocks to talk about their strange find.

'But if poteen is being smuggled down from the mountains,' said Cowlick, 'what's it doing in the sea?'

'And in a bottle from the Castle Spa,' said Tapser.

'Sure you get poteen in any sort of bottle,' argued Roisin. 'Daddy always keeps a drop of it in the house, and it's in a 7-Up bottle.'

'What does he keep it for?' asked Tapser.

'Some of it goes into the plum pudding at Christmas,' Rachel told him. 'And if we've a sick calf, a dash of it in the milk can be a great help.'

'But I thought it was illegal?'

'So it is,' said Cowlick. 'But we're only talking about a wee drop of it for emergencies. Peppi was talking about a big shipment, and that's definitely against the law.'

Tapser broke a stalk of seaweed and threw the stump away for Prince to fetch. Suddenly he said, 'How about going up to the Castle Spa? I've an idea.'

'If you're thinking of taking up Max's invitation, forget it,' Rachel advised him. 'When he says "Come when I'm not busy," he means don't come. He's always busy.'

'It's not him I want to see,' Tapser replied. 'Come on.'

On the way they stopped at the little harbour. Fishing boats rested idly by the quayside, and a small cargo ship was taking on crates of spa water. American visitors were finding the harbour very 'quaint' and asking each other to hold their bottles of spa water while they got photographs taken of themselves with the harbour in the background.

'You know what I was wondering?' said Tapser. 'Who's to say what's in those bottles?'

'Do you mean it might be poteen?' whispered Rachel.

'Why not? Doesn't it look just like water?'

They all studied the posing tourists and the bottles they clutched in their arms. Then they looked at each other.

'I suppose it could be poteen,' said Cowlick, and the others nodded.

'But why?' asked Rachel. 'Why should it be poteen?'

'Didn't you hear Peppi say the police can't find out how it's getting out of the glen?' said Tapser. 'Isn't that the ideal way to do it ... openly, as spa water. Nobody would know the difference.'

'That's true,' Roisin agreed. 'They could take it out by the bus-load.'

'All right,' said Cowlick. 'It's worth investigating. Let's go up to the Castle Spa and see what we can find out.'

It was a short, steep climb up from the Low Road and all of them including Prince were panting when they got to the forecourt of the Castle Spa. There they joined the tourists queueing for the shops where the water was sold in bottles. As they moved forward, Cowlick pointed out the sign. It said: '*Maxwell's Well Makes Well*'.

Tapser smiled. 'He has a funny sense of humour all right.' He looked up at the tall, turreted building that rose high above the shops out of the side of the glen. The castle itself was marked 'Private' and two big alsatian dogs roamed the grounds behind a high wire fence. 'And it's a funny sort of hotel. I don't see any guests.'

'That's because Max doesn't run it as an hotel any more,' said Cowlick. 'I told you that.'

They were in one of the shops now, and while the tourists bought their bottles of water the four of them edged up to where the supplies were stacked on shelves like large bottles of white lemonade.

When he thought no one was looking, Tapser took down a bottle and unscrewed the cap, but before he could sniff it, a strong hand clamped on his shoulder and a man with a foreign accent inquired if he was going to buy it.

'I . . . I'd like to,' replied Tapser somewhat nervously.

'But we haven't got the money,' said Roisin, coming to his aid.

'Then you have no business in here,' growled the man.

'But Mr. van Weshal said we could come,' Tapser protested.

The man ignored him and marched them towards the door. There they met Prince and, sensing that the man was being distinctly unfriendly to his young master, the collie bared his teeth in a snarl.

The man released Tapser and ordered, 'Get out, all of you. And take that dog with you. It is not hygienic to have animals in a shop. And do not come back in here unless you wish to buy something.'

Outside, Tapser pulled his jacket back into place and remarked, 'They're not very friendly, are they?'

'They're like that,' Cowlick told him. 'Max is the same. It's all business and they don't stand for any nonsense.'

'No, they sure don't, do they?' said a tourist who had seen what happened. She had pink hair and matching glasses, and it was obvious she was an American.

Her husband gave Tapser's red hair a friendly wigging and said, 'I thought all you Irishmen had black curly hair.'

'Hugh Rua had red hair too,' said Tapser defensively.

'Oh yeah, Red Hugh, the Highwayman of the Glen,' said the man. 'We read about him in our guide book. Well, maybe it's the red-haired ones that are wild. Say, why did that guy throw you out anyhow?'

Tapser shrugged. 'Because we were looking at the bottles.'

'You mean to say he threw you out just because of that?' said the woman. 'Well, here, have one of ours. You're more than welcome.'

They all protested, but the woman added, 'Go on, why not for goodness sakes. After all, it's only water.'

So it was, as they found when they tested the bottle on the way back into town.

'So much for that idea,' remarked Roisin.

'Well it could have been poteen,' said Tapser. 'And Max could have been smuggling it out that way. After all, there was poteen in the other bottle we found.'

'Well if Max isn't using his bottles to smuggle poteen,

who is?' asked Cowlick.

'And where is it coming from?' wondered Roisin.

'Peppi seems to think there's a big still hidden away somewhere up in the mountains, and that's where it's coming from,' said Rachel.

'But how come one of the bottles ended up in the sea?' said Cowlick. 'That's the funny part of it.'

'What do you really think of Peppi?' Tapser asked.

'We like him,' replied Rachel.

'But we sometimes wonder about him,' said Roisin.

'You mean the woollen gloves?'

'I suppose so,' said Roisin.

'You don't think he's bringing it down from the mountains, do you?'

Cowlick laughed. 'Tapser, would you give over. A minute ago you were saying Max was the smuggler. Now it's poor oul' Peppi.'

'Still,' said Tapser, 'he would be in an ideal position to smuggle it, wouldn't he? I mean, he could collect it without raising any suspicion.'

'He does seem to know an awful lot about poteen,' Roisin agreed.

'That's right,' said Rachel. 'You heard him saying that whenever Hugh Rua is supposed to be seen, it means there's a shipment on the way.'

'It's a funny business that about Hugh Rua,' said Tapser. 'I wonder where we could find out more about him?'

'What for?' asked Cowlick.

'Well, if Peppi was right about the poteen smugglers being on the move, maybe he was right about the phantom too.'

'Mr. Stephenson could probably tell us more about

him,' Roisin suggested.' He owns the Highwayman Inn.'

'That's right,' said Rachel. 'He has a coach he displays every year at the show. But we better go home for our dinner first.'

After dinner they made their way back into town and out to where the High Road sloped down to the sea. On the corner where the two roads met, stood the Highwayman public house.

'Talk of the devil,' exclaimed Tapser. 'There's Peppi.'

'And there's a police car parked outside,' said Cowlick. 'I wonder what's going on?'

Peppi had put a nosebag on his horse and was casually watching the comings and goings.

'What are you doing here?' he asked them.

'We thought Mr. Stephenson could tell us more about Hugh Rua,' Tapser told him.

'You're not the only ones,' said Peppi.

'Why, what's going on?' asked Roisin.

'It's a raid. The police seem to think Sam knows something about this phantom business. They're in there now talking to him and Blind Jack.'

'Blind Jack?' asked Tapser. 'Who's he?'

'Jack's his handyman,' Cowlick told him. 'He minds the coach and that sort of thing.'

Tapser was studying the sign above the door portraying Hugh Rua's celebrated coach robbery, when the police suddenly emerged and drove off. Mr. Stephenson, a big burly man with rolled-up shirt sleeves and a white apron, came to the door a moment later.

'What's the matter, Sam?' inquired Peppi. 'Are you in trouble?'

'It would take more than a visit by the polis to get

me into trouble,' laughed Mr. Stephenson. 'I've nothing to hide.'

'Can I show them the coach?'

'Sure why not? There's not a soul in the place now — not after that carry-on.'

Out in the back yard, they found that Mr. Stephenson was something of a collector. He had a pony-trap, a jaunting car and various other horse-drawn vehicles, but the pride of his collection was a coach that was being polished by a man in a leather apron.

'That,' said Mr. Stephenson with a wave of his hand, 'is the *Londonderry Mail.* She went all the way from Belfast to Derry.'

It was a really magnificent coach. Its wheels and central shaft were painted red, while the lower part of the body was yellow and the top part black. These, Mr. Stephenson informed them, were the coaching colours of the day.

'You also had the Southern mail coach running between Dublin and Cork, and the Northern mail coach between Dublin and Belfast,' he told them. 'And a lot more.'

'Why did they call them mail coaches?' Rachel asked him.

'Because they carried the mail as well as passengers — you know, letters and things. And believe it or not, that made a big difference in their time-keeping.'

'How come?' asked Cowlick.

Mr. Stephenson scratched his head as if wondering how to explain it. 'Well, prior to that the stage coaches were notorious for their bad time-keeping. The roads were bad, and sometimes the coaches would get stuck in the mud or break a wheel. Apart from that, there were often long delays at the coaching inns when some of the passengers, and maybe even the coachmen, overstayed their welcome.'

'You mean drinking,' said Roisin, who thought that as a publican Mr. Stephenson might be avoiding the word.

'Mmm ... more a case of drinking to excess I'd say, and to the exclusion of the feelings of other passengers who were anxious to be on their way. Then, in 1784 a separate Post Office was established for Ireland, and four or five years later mail coaches, like the ones they had in England, began to operate in addition to the stage coaches.'

'How did that improve things?' asked Cowlick.

'Part of the new scheme was that the mail should be timed at each stage,' said Mr. Stephenson. 'That meant the mail coaches didn't delay, or if they did they had to make it up before the next stage.' He was staring straight ahead now as if he was seeing it all in his mind's eye. 'Somehow I'd say there was great competition between them and the stage coaches. You can just imagine them racing each other ... maybe four or six horses to each coach, galloping madly as the drivers urged them on, people hanging on by their finger-nails to the seats on the roofs of the swaying coaches. Aye, them were the days. The golden age of the stage coach.'

Somehow Rachel couldn't help thinking that travelling by coach must have been a very uncomfortable experience, even if they did arrive at their destination on time. 'But what about the *Londonderry Mail?*' she asked him. 'Can you tell us more about it?'

Mr. Stephenson eased his large frame down on to an aluminium beer barrel, and looking at his own coach, continued, 'At first the mail coaches only operated between Dublin and Cork and Dublin and Belfast, but gradually they spread out. By 1805 they were going down to Waterford, over to Sligo and up as far as Derry. It wasn't long before they were operating out of Belfast to Antrim, Ballymena, Ballymoney and Coleraine, then on to Derry that way. That was the route of the *Londonderry Mail.*'

'How many horses would it have had?' asked Tapser, who was trying to imagine it going up the Old Coach Road near his home at Ballymena.

'Probably four. From the information I've been able to dig up, it was expected to travel between five and six miles an hour. The average fare was three old pence per mile if you were sitting on top; five old pence if you were inside. The journey to Derry took 17 hours in 1811, and the time-table was arranged so that the local merchants had seven hours in which to reply to incoming mail before the coach returned to Belfast.'

'And what about highwaymen?' asked Tapser. 'Mr. Stockman says there were a lot of them.'

'Indeed there were,' agreed Mr. Stephenson. 'That's why the coaches had to have armed guards.'

'What sort of guns did they use?' asked Cowlick.

'Oh, they'd have pistols, and a brass blunderbuss.'

'Mr. Stockman told me the highwaymen sometimes

used a blunderbuss too,' said Tapser. 'He said it was a big gun with a wide end on it like a trumpet.'

Mr. Stephenson nodded. 'So they did, and sometimes armed dragoons — that's soldiers on horseback — had to escort the coaches through mountainous or remote areas where highwaymen were likely to strike.'

Anxious to turn the conversation around to Hugh Rua, Tapser asked him if he knew anything about actual robberies.

'Well, I know they weren't always carried out by one highwayman as you might imagine,' said Mr. Stephenson. 'The Enniskillen mail, for example, was robbed at Dunshaughlin in Co. Meath by no less than fourteen armed men. *The Cock of the North* — now wasn't that a fine name for a coach? — it was held up near Newry by ten men. After robbing the passengers, they also stole the driver's whip so that he wouldn't be able to catch up with them or raise the alarm too soon, I suppose. And then there was the Limerick mail. It was robbed by 13 armed men near Maryborough, or Portlaoise, as they call it now. They even stole the horses!'

'I bet Hugh Rua was the only one who ever stole a coach,' said Cowlick.

'The only one I ever heard of,' agreed Mr. Stephenson. 'But then he had a reason for doing that.'

'Did he really exist?' asked Tapser.

'Well I heard about him from my father and he heard about him from his father. Don't forget, it wasn't until the 1830s that the isolation of the glens was ended with the building of the coast road. So who's to say Hugh Rua didn't try to end that isolation? Or that he didn't exist — just because you can't find the story in your history books?'

'And is this really the coach he stole?' asked Tapser.

'Well, not the real one,' admitted Mr. Stephenson. 'It's a reproduction. But it's the same, right down to the last detail. Isn't that right, Jack?'

The man in the leather apron turned and grunted agreement. He was rather sourly, Tapser thought, or maybe just shy in the fashion of some country people.

'Jack looks after my coaches here,' explained Mr. Stephenson. 'We call him Blind Jack after a famous coachbuilder of the last century.'

Jack managed a smile as if to say he didn't mind the nickname, and continued polishing.

'But be warned,' whispered Mr. Stephenson as he helped them into the coach. 'Don't damage the paintwork, or you'll find he has a sharper eye in his head than I have!'

They laughed and promised to be careful.

'Do you ever take the coach out?' asked Tapser.

' 'Deed we do,' said Mr. Stephenson. 'Any parade we have, it's in it.'

'Do you have horses then?'

'That I have. Sure how do you think I farm some of the fields up here on the side of the glen? You'd never get a tractor up into them.'

'The Legend of Hugh Rua must be a great tourist attraction,' remarked Roisin, fishing for information.

'Great,' he agreed. 'They all come up here to see the coach.' He paused, then added, 'You know, I was wondering if it would be worthwhile during the summer, running the *Londonderry Mail* on excursions along the High Road as far as the memorial and back.'

'Come for a ride in the phantom coach,' said Cowlick. 'That would be a great attraction.'

'Ah, well now, phantom highwaymen are something else,' said Mr. Stephenson. 'You'll have the polis on me again if you talk like that.'

'But there is a lot of talk about the ghost of Hugh Rua being seen on the High Road,' Roisin reminded him, 'and what it means.'

'Coaches and highwaymen have always been the subject of ghost stories,' said Mr. Stephenson. 'And their ghosts are always said to be some kind of omen, usually bad.' He leaned forward so that his head was now sticking in through the open window. 'Down in Cork there's an old legend about a phantom coach. They call it the Death Coach, for the story goes that when it drives round a house at midnight, with the coachman's whip cracking loudly, it's a sure sign of death.'

Lowering his voice, he went on ...

Still rolling and rumbling, that sound
Making nearer and nearer approach;
Do I tremble, or is it the ground? -
Lord, save us! - what is it? - a coach! -

A coach! but that coach has no head;
And the horses are headless as it;
Of the driver the same may be said
And the passengers inside it who sit.

Both the poem and the way Mr. Stephenson said it were so scarey that the four of them suddenly felt a great urge to get out, and ignoring the metal step below the door, they jumped to the ground.

Mr. Stephenson closed the door after them, and with a wink to Blind Jack, continued, 'But you need go no further than the vanishing lake to find another story of a phantom coach.'

'What coach was that?' asked Roisin.

'It belonged to Colonel Jack McNeill. As you know, the lake sometimes appears on one side of the road, then on the other.'

They all knew about the vanishing lake, or Lough-areema, as it was more properly called, on the mountain between Cushendun and Ballycastle, and when they nodded, he went on.

'Well, it was in 1898 that it happened. They say there was a terrible storm on the mountain, but Col. McNeill was anxious to get to Ballycastle to catch the train to Belfast. There were no walls at the side of the road at that time, and the lake had risen so far the road was flooded. Whether the coachman missed the road or the horses panicked, nobody knows. But whatever happened the coach careered off into the lake, and both the men and the horses were drowned. Sometimes they say, you can still hear the coach rumbling down the road and screeching as it goes into the water.'

As they thought about that, Mr. Stephenson lowered his voice again and continued . . .

Onest before the morning light
A horseman will come riding
Round and round the fairy lough
And no one there to see . . .

'Who wrote that?' asked Tapser.

'Moira O'Neill, poetess of the glens.' Mr. Stephenson took a deep breath. 'There are those who won't go past the lake on a stormy night, for they know that if the two horses put their heads up out of the water their hair will turn white!'

'That's silly,' said Roisin.

'Anyway,' said Rachel, 'Colonel McNeill wasn't a highwayman.'

'No, but Redmond O'Hanlon was. He was a famous highwayman down in south Armagh. Tradition has it that his ghost still haunts the highways and by-ways that were the scenes of his adventures.'

'You're just trying to scare us,' said Cowlick.

Mr. Stephenson laughed and ruffled his cow's-lick curl. 'Not really. All I'm saying is, there are a lot of these stories, and maybe you shouldn't take all this talk about the ghost of Hugh Rua too seriously.'

They walked out to the road.

'How was Hugh Rua captured?' asked Tapser.

Mr. Stephenson shrugged. 'A highwayman always had a price on his head, and there was always somebody willing to collect it. Sometimes the informer would pour water into the highwayman's guns, and with his powder wet he wasn't able to offer much resistance when the soldiers came. That's what happened Thomas Archer, the Ballymena highwayman, and another one down in Waterford called William Crotty. Who knows? Maybe that was the way Hugh Rua was captured too.'

In spite of his extensive knowledge of coaches and highwaymen, Mr. Stephenson hadn't really told them much more about Hugh Rua than they already knew, but before they could ask him anything else, he stopped and said, 'Anyway, enough about highwaymen. Tell me, are you coming to the ceili tonight?'

'We forgot all about it,' said Rachel.

'Well, remind your people it's on tonight. It's being sponsored by the Castle Spa, and we're going to have a whale of a time.'

4 SEEING THINGS

Back home, they found that the barley had been cut and the bales were being collected from the fields.

'Well, who's doing the smuggling now?' asked Roisin. She had plaited a straw bobbin and was putting Rachel's hair up in a pony-tail.

'I don't know,' said Tapser. 'But I still think Max and Peppi are tied up with it somehow.'

'What more can we do?' asked Cowlick.

'Well there are two things I'd like to do,' said Tapser. 'I'd like to have a look at Max's bottling plant. And I'd like to see inside Peppi's caravan.'

'You'd be asking for trouble if you tried that,' warned Rachel.

'She's right,' said Cowlick.

'What if we did it when they weren't looking?' said Tapser.

'And when might that be?' asked Roisin.

'How about tonight, when they're at the ceili? Peppi said he'd be there. And if the Castle Spa is sponsoring it, Max will probably be there too.'

The others looked at each other. They were beginning to wonder about their red-haired cousin and his bright ideas.

By the time it came to go to the ceili, however, Tapser had convinced the others that if they wanted to find out who was behind this smuggling business, Max and Peppi would have to be investigated.

The ceili was already under way when they arrived at the Highwayman. There was no sign of Peppi, but they were relieved to hear Max doing his party-piece inside. Peering through a window, they saw him standing, glass in hand, singing a verse of the *Ballad of Hugh Rua.*

They hung him on the High Road
In chains he swung and dried,
But still they say that in the night
Some do see him ride.
They see him with his blunderbuss
In the midnight chill,
Along the High Road of the glen
Rides Hugh Rua still . . . .

Rachel nipped into tell her mother and father that they were going down town, and as everyone joined in the chorus the four of them stole away.

It was almost dark and the Castle Spa jutted up into the purple sky like a giant finger of chalk.

Crouching behind a clump of bushes, they scanned the high wire fence.

'How are we going to get in?' whispered Cowlick.

Two shadowy figures came bounding down the inside of the fence.

'The alsatians,' warned Roisin.

'Oh-oh, I don't like this one bit,' whispered Rachel.

'You don't have to go in', Tapser told her. 'I've got an idea.'

'Here we go again,' sighed Roisin. 'Another bright idea.'

'Would you keep quiet,' said Cowlick, 'and listen.'

'You and Rachel take Prince,' Tapser told Roisin. 'Go away up to the far end of the castle grounds. And don't worry about keeping quiet. Make sure the alsatians follow you. They'll go mad to get out to you when you have the dog.'

'And what will we do?' asked Cowlick.

'When the alsatians are at the far end we can get in over the fence.'

'And then what?'

'We'll make for that cluster of out-buildings and see if we can find the bottling plant. Where's the best place to get over the fence?'

'There's a sycamore tree down there to our left,' said Cowlick. 'I think we could swing over in from that.'

'Great.' Tapser turned to the girls and told them, 'We'd better take the torch in case we need it. Off you go, and whatever you do make sure you keep the alsatians busy.'

'We'll do our best,' Roisin assured him. 'But be careful. Alsatians can be very vicious.'

Taking Prince with them, Roisin and Rachel ran crouching up along the fence. Immediately the alsatians were over to them, barking loudly and jumping up against the wire. Prince barked back, but Roisin held on to him as she ran and the alsatians followed them.

When they had disappeared into the gloom and the barking had become more distant, Tapser and Cowlick dashed over to the fence. They helped each other up the sycamore tree, made their way out along the lowest branch, and dropped down the other side.

Pausing only to cast an anxious glance in the direction of the barking, they sprinted towards the out-buildings.

'Now where do we go?' panted Tapser when they had nipped inside.

'Anywhere but here,' cried Cowlick. 'The alsatians are coming! Run for it!'

They turned to run but tripped over a bale of straw and fell headlong. Scrambling to their feet, they clawed their way up a large pile of bales and found the top just as the two alsatians jumped up, snarling and snapping at their heels.

'What are we going to do?' whispered Cowlick.

'Get down in between the bales,' advised Tapser. 'Hurry, somebody's coming.'

'What is going on?' asked a deep voice in a foreign accent.

'I think there must be an intruder in the barn,' replied another. 'Perhaps we should switch on the lights.'

'No, no. If someone has got in, we will find him.'

Tapser and Cowlick squeezed themselves down in between the bales as far as they could. Their hearts were thumping after the narrow escape they had had with the alsatians and with the fear that they were now going to be caught.

'I will hold the dogs,' said the man with the deep voice. 'See if you can find out what has made them so excited.'

The other man began climbing up the bales, but as he neared the top Tapser and Cowlick heard something

flutter above their heads. Almost immediately the man fell back, screaming with fright, and the dogs began barking again.

Cautiously they peeped over the bales to see what was going on. They could just make out Whaler, who was holding the alsatians, ducking his head. Then they heard him laugh and say to the other man, 'Get up you fool, it is only bats. Come, we had better put the dogs in. The lorry will be here soon.'

The other man picked himself up. They could see it was Scamp.

As Whaler led the two dogs away, he was still laughing, and saying, 'Bats! What did you think it was? A monster?'

Scamp, however, wasn't amused.

In their hiding-place between the bales, Tapser and Cowlick heaved a huge sigh of relief. Across the yard they saw a door open and a shaft of light shine out until it was closed again.

'Whew, that was a close shave,' gasped Cowlick.

'You can say that again,' said Tapser. 'Lucky for us we disturbed the bats.'

'Did you hear your man screaming?' said Cowlick. 'he must have got a right fright.'

Tapser smiled to himself, and added, 'I wonder why they didn't want to put on the lights?'

'Listen,' said Cowlick, 'there's a car coming.'

Easing themselves back down behind the bales, they watched as a vehicle drove into the yard.

'It must be the lorry they were talking about,' whispered Tapser.

'And it hasn't any lights on either,' Cowlick observed.

Another shaft of light cut across the yard lighting up the lorry for a moment, and they could see it was loaded with crates of bottles. Shadowy figures gathered around the lorry. Somebody propped open a shed door, and men hurried in with the crates. In a short time the lorry was unloaded and the door closed again, leaving the yard in darkness. The lorry started up and drove away, and suddenly the yard was deserted.

'Come on,' said Tapser, 'there's something funny going on here. Let's see what we can find out before they let the dogs out again.'

Quietly they climbed down to the yard and ran across to the door. They listened. There wasn't a sound. They opened the door and stepped inside. There was no one about, and they tip-toed along a dimly-lit passage-way. Somewhere ahead they could the hear the clink of bottles. Following the noise, they made their way down steps and around corners, until they found themselves looking down into a large cavern. In the middle of the floor was a big machine in which bottles were whirled around to be filled, capped and labelled, in a dazzling display of movement and precision. Elsewhere in the cavern, workmen were piling up crates which presumably they had brought down from the lorry.

As Tapser and Cowlick tried to take it all in, they were amazed to hear the sound of a boat's engine, and switching their gaze to a cave beyond the bottling plant, they saw a boat nudging its way in.

Opening an iron gate, Whaler and Scamp went out to meet it, and when it was moored tightly the boatmen handed them up crate after crate of bottles which they brought back and placed on the floor of the large cavern.

'That's one of Max's lobster boats,' said Cowlick.

'Well they haven't been catching lobsters, that's for sure,' said Tapser. 'Do you think they're the smugglers?'

'I don't know. But it's all very strange.'

'You can say that again. Come on. We'd better get out of here before they come back up.'

There was no sign of the alsatians, so they raced across the darkened grounds and a few minutes later dropped down outside the wire fence. Roisin and Rachel, who had been hiding nearby, rushed over to meet them, and Prince barked a greeting.

'Quiet boy,' urged Tapser, and they all hunkered down and looked back to see if anyone had heard. No one had, and they hurried away.

As they walked back through the town, Tapser and Cowlick told the girls what they had seen.

'We were terrified the alsatians were going to tear you to pieces,' said Roisin. 'We couldn't keep them up there any longer.'

'They would have too, only for the bats.'

The girls laughed when they heard about that.

'Poor Scamp,' giggled Rachel. 'He must have got a terrible fright.'

'Aye,' laughed Cowlick. 'I think they flew into his face.'

'Yugh,' shivered Roisin. 'I wouldn't fancy that.'

'Bats are harmless,' said Rachel.

'I know. But still. It's the thought of it.'

'Well, they saved our bacon anyway,' said Cowlick. 'They're very dangerous dogs, them alsatians.'

'Aye, and I didn't fancy the thought of Whaler getting his big hands on us either,' said Tapser.

'Do you think Max is involved in this smuggling business then?' asked Roisin.

'There's something very funny going on over there,' said Tapser.

'Why do you say that?' asked Rachel.

'Well for a start,' Cowlick told her, 'that lorry had no lights on.'

'And Whaler didn't want to put the lights on in the yard,' recalled Tapser.

'I wonder why?' said Roisin.

'Unless it was a lorry-load of poteen they were smuggling down from the mountains,' said Cowlick.

'Maybe they were just empties that had been collected,' suggested Rachel.

'Then why bring them in at this time of night?' argued Tapser. 'And with the lights switched off. No, there's something funny about the way they were acting.'

'Not to mention the boat,' Cowlick reminded them.

'That is funny,' Rachel agreed. 'Do you think it was poteen too?'

'Sure they wouldn't be bringing poteen down from the mountains that way,' asserted Roisin.

'And it was properly bottled and all,' Tapser recalled.

'Just like the bottles from the machine.'

'Well the mountainy men wouldn't be bottling it like that,' said Roisin, 'from what I know of them.'

' Do you think that machine could be the big still Peppi was talking about?' asked Tapser.

'Not at all,' said Cowlick. 'They don't make poteen in a contraption like that. It would have to have a fire and barrels and all sorts of things, and anyway you'd smell it.'

'Do you still think we should have a look at Peppi's caravan?' asked Roisin.

'Why not?' said Tapser. 'Sure maybe he's involved in this business too. He could be the contact man or anything up the mountain.'

'Could he have something to do with the appearance of Hugh Rua on the High Road?' asked Cowlick.

'Well, as you say, he does seem to know a lot about this poteen business,' said Tapser.

'But the police seem to think it's Sam Stephenson or Blind Jack that are behind that,' Rachel reminded them. 'And they do know an awful lot about coaches and highwaymen.'

That was true, the others had to admit, so they continued to turn the various possibilities over in their minds as they made their way back up to the Highwayman Inn.

They could tell by the music and the general sound of merriment that the ceili was still in full swing, but there was still no sign of Peppi's caravan so they sat down on the low wall and wondered what to do.

Below them, the waves glistened in the moonlight as they rolled in and crashed against the rocks. They were almost like phantom white horses, thought Tapser, and as he looked down he couldn't help feeling how strong and powerful they sounded, and how dark and lonely a place the beach seemed at night. 'Are there many caves along the cliffs?' he asked.

'There's a lot of them all right,' Cowlick told him.'But I never knew one of them went in under the Castle Spa.'

'Well, we're going to have to do a bit of exploring the first chance we get,' said Tapser.

Cowlick glanced around. 'I wonder where Peppi is? He said he would be here.'

'Did you ever think that's a funny name for his caravan?' said Rachel. 'Pandora's Box.'

'It's a name given to a box full of all sorts of nick-nacks,' Roisin told her.

'You mean, like mammy's box of buttons and things?'

'I suppose so.'

'But where does it come from?' asked Cowlick.

'From mythology,' said Tapser, to everyone's surprise, and he went on to explain, 'My father bought a book once, about mythology. He wanted to read about Diana the huntress. And I remember there was something in it about Pandora.'

'That's right,' said Roisin. 'I looked it up in my encyclopaedia. It's a Greek story.'

'You didn't tell me that,' said Rachel reproachfully.

'Well I'm telling you now, amn't I? It says the gods quarrelled, and one of them decided to send something down to the men which would cause trouble. So he made a woman.'

'Huh, the cheek of them,' said Rachel, 'suggesting that women are the ones that cause trouble!'

'Go on,' urged Cowlick impatiently. 'What else did it say?'

'She was called Pandora, which means all-gifted, for the gods and goddesses gave her gifts to bring with her, beauty, charm, and the art of flattery. But one present was a special box which she was forbidden to open. Of course, curiosity got the better of her, and when she opened it a swarm of winged monsters flew out. They were disease, anger, revenge . . . all the curses that left men miserable.'

'What did she do then?' asked Tapser.

'She tried to close the box, but it was too late. They had all escaped and flown over the world, and only Hope was left.'

'Oh, I don't like the sound of that,' shuddered Rachel.

'I wonder if it's Peppi's idea of a joke?' said Tapser.

'How do you mean?' asked Cowlick.

'Well, maybe his coach or caravan or whatever you call it has some dark secret, and by calling himself Pandora and Company he's really telling everybody about it, knowing they won't understand.'

'A funny sort of joke,' said Rachel. 'But you could be right. He could be in the business of transporting poteen. Then his Pandora's Box really would be full of curses, wouldn't it? For people talk about the curse of drink, don't they?'

'Right,' said Roisin, 'that settles it. We've got to have a look inside his caravan. But where is he?'

They got up and wandered over to the window. Cowlick pushed himself up on the window-sill and looked in over the frosted part of the glass. 'Peppi's inside,' he announced.

'Then his caravan must be out at the back,' said Roisin. 'Come on, now's as good a time as any.'

In the yard they found that Peppi had unhitched his horse and given it a nosebag of food. The caravan was parked nearby.

'You two stay here and keep on eye out for Peppi,' whispered Roisin. 'We'll have a look inside the caravan. Come on, Rachel.'

'Are you sure you don't want us to do it? ' asked Tapser.

'Sure,' said Roisin, taking the torch from him. 'Come on, Rachel.' Seeing her hesitate, she added, 'Don't be silly that story about Pandora was only something the Greeks made up. Hurry.'

Tapser and Cowlick watched from the back door of the inn as the girls climbed aboard. Rachel positioned herself at the driver's seat to keep a look-out too, while Roisin made her way inside.

Closing the door behind her, Roisin switched on her torch. The section behind the driver's seat, she could see, was Peppi's living quarters. There was an iron stove, a bunk-bed and a small chest of drawers. There was no sign of any bottles, but she came across a tin box. In spite of her assurance to Rachel about the story of Pandora being made up, her hands trembled as she lifted the box wondering what was in it. Gingerly she opened the lid a little bit, then a bit more, and when it was opened fully, she found, not a swarm of little winged monsters, but something else that made her gasp in disbelief.

'Rachel,' she whispered, 'look at this.'

Seeing Rachel scramble inside, Tapser and Cowlick rushed over to find out what was happening.

'Look,' said Roisin as they put their heads in around the door. She was holding a card up to the light. It was headed: 'Her Majesty's Customs and Excise. Investigation Branch.' And below that was a photograph of Peppi.

'That means Peppi is a secret agent,' said Tapser.

'That's right,' said a voice behind them, and turning around they came face to face with Peppi!

5 THE PHANTOM OF HUGH RUA

For a moment time seemed to stand still. Peppi looked at them and they looked at Peppi. None of them spoke. What could they say? They had been caught red-handed.

Then Tapser said. 'I'm sorry, Peppi. This was all my idea.'

'And mine,' said Roisin.

'We thought you were bringing poteen down from the mountains,' said Cowlick.

'Me? Smuggling poteen?' laughed Peppi. 'So you're on the track of the poteen-smugglers too?'

'We thought we were,' said Rachel.

'Frankly, Peppi,' Roisin said, 'Rachel and I thought you were very suspicious.'

'Suspicious? In what way?'

'Well, it was your woollen gloves really,' admitted Rachel. 'We felt you were hiding something.'

'Well now, hold it,' said Peppi. 'Before we go any

further, we must make a deal.'

'What sort of a deal?' asked Cowlick.

'You must promise not to give me away.'

'We won't blow your cover, really,' Tapser assured him, anxious to make amends and using a phrase he had heard on television.

'I'm glad,' said Peppi. 'Now, you say you're looking for the smugglers. So am I. What do you say we join forces?'

Nothing could have pleased them better, and they heartily agreed.

'All right then. But remember, secrecy is most important. You mustn't discuss my activities with anyone. All right? Now, I can't talk to you here. I've work to do, and you wouldn't know who might be listening. So I tell you what. Tomorrow's Sunday. I'll call for you after dinner if you like, and you can come up the mountains with me. We can talk then.,

When the girls had gone to bed, Tapser and Cowlick sat up late talking.

'This is a funny one, isn't it?' said Tapser.

'How do you mean?'

'Well, when we were investigating *The Legend of the Golden Key* last summer we knew it was something to do with treasure. You know, something solid. But this business is different.'

'In what way?'

'I just wonder sometimes if it's all in our imagination. I mean, poteen-makers and smugglers and phantom highwaymen. It's like looking for the will-o'-the-wisp in the Cottonbog back home.'

'If it's just our imagination,' said Cowlick, 'then Peppi

and the police are in the same boat. And talking of boats, don't forget what we saw at the Castle Spa. That needs some explaining.'

'But if Max and his men are involved in smuggling poteen,' said Tapser, 'what's that got to do with the phantom highwayman?'

'I don't know, except Peppi said that when Hugh Rua is seen on the High Road it's a sure sign there's a shipment on the way.'

'But what is it that's been seen on the High Road?' Tapser wondered. 'It can't be a phantom. Unless, of course, the police are right and Sam Stephenson and Blind Jack have something to do with it.'

'Why should they?'

Tapser shrugged. 'Maybe they're trying to get publicity for the Highwayman Inn. Remember, Mr. Stephenson said they were thinking of taking the coach up as far as the memorial on day-trips. Maybe they're even in league with the poteen-smugglers.'

'Why then should they draw attention to the fact that the poteen is on the way?'

'I don't suppose it could be Peppi doing it to raise the alarm or something?'

'On that oul' horse of his?' laughed Cowlick. 'You must be joking. I think it's time you got some sleep.'

'You can sleep if you like,' said Tapser. 'But I'm going to keep an eye on the High Road. If anything appears on it tonight, I want to see it.'

So saying, Tapser went over to the window and settled down for a long wait.

'Well, I'm going to bed,' said Cowlick, turning off the light. 'If you see anything give me a shout.'

Peering out into the night, Tapser could see that a

breeze had sprung up. It brought occasional clouds across the moon and moulded the rowanberry trees on the side of the glen into ever-changing shapes and shadows. Up on the rim of the glen, scraggy hawthorn bushes seemed to have turned their backs to the wind and sea. As the night wore on, he became tired and sleepy and sometimes he imagined that the clouds looked like faces, or horses, or that the bushes looked like flowing capes.

After what seemed an eternity, the clock downstairs chimed four times. Tapser was still sitting at the window, trying to keep his eyes open and focussed on the High Road, yet knowing he was fighting a losing battle. Suddenly he sat upright and shook his head to clear the sleep from his mind. It couldn't be true, he told himself. He must be dreaming. But no, there it was! The unmistakeable outline of a horse and rider, galloping along the High Road, the rider's cape billowing out behind him as he urged his horse on to greater speed.

Tapser rushed over to rouse Cowlick. 'Quick. Quick.'

'What's the matter?' mumbled Cowlick in his sleep.

'It's the phantom highwayman, up on the High Road. Come on.'

Cowlick swung his legs out and sat on the edge of the bed. He was groggy with sleep. 'I'm coming,' he said. His eyes were still closed and he put his head in his hands and yawned.

Tapser, however, was already on his way. Slipping out the back door, he paused for a moment with the idea of getting Prince. Nothing stirred, and afraid that he might waken the two sheepdogs, he hurried on up the back fields. Cowlick hadn't appeared yet, but he knew he wouldn't be far behind.

Strange as it may seem, Tapser wasn't scared as he

climbed the side of the glen by the light of the moon. Had he stopped to think about it, he would have been, but the truth was he was too excited. As he scrambled up through the bushes and scrub, there was only one thing in his mind, and that was to get to the High Road with all possible speed in the hope of catching a glimpse of Hugh Rua.

When he emerged up through the ravine on to the rim of the glen, the horse and rider were nowhere to be seen. He scanned the High Road towards the glistening sea and to the dark mass of the mountains. It was deserted. The only sounds to disturb the stillness were the waves breaking in the distance and the panting of his own breath.

He looked around for the bronze memorial, but couldn't find it. He looked back, expecting to see Cowlick any minute, and when there was no sign of him he walked along the road, ready at a moment's notice to jump over the ditch if the phantom rider should appear again. Maybe it had just been his imagination, he thought. But no, he assured himself, he had seen it.

Pulling his jacket collar up around his neck, he kept walking until he came to a fork in the road. There he stopped and wondered if the rider had gone up left into the mountains, or right, down into the glen. Then he heard voices and took cover behind the ditch. Now for the first time he wished Prince was with him. And where was Cowlick? He just hoped he hadn't gone back to sleep.

Cautiously he peered over the ditch. The voices were coming from the shadows on the road down to the glen. Crossing the road he made his way down along the back of the ditch on the far side. The voices got louder, and he could now make out a lorry parked in off the road. The men were looking at one of the wheels, and he got the impression that it had a puncture. Finally, one of them gave the wheel a kick and they all walked off down the road.

'The smugglers!' said Tapser to himself, and when they had disappeared he climbed over the ditch and pulled himself up on to the punctured wheel. 'Just as I thought,' he said. 'Bottles.'

Taking one, he hopped back down, unscrewed the cap and put it to his mouth. The minute he did so, he realized it was poteen, but this time he didn't get a chance to spit it out. Voices told him the men were coming back and he got such a surprise that he swallowed it. The poteen seemed to burn all the way down into his stomach. Suddenly he felt like getting sick. He also felt dizzy. He managed to put back the bottle and held his head. The men were coming closer. He must get away.

Clutching his stomach, he staggered back up the road. Everything was swirling around before his eyes ... the road, the ditches, the hills, the moon.

'There he is!' he heard a voice shout. He tried to run,

but somehow the road seemed to get steeper and steeper and he didn't have the strength to climb it. It was like a nightmare. Next moment, he felt a hand grabbing him by the shoulder, and he knew he was caught.

It was then that the strangest thing of all happened. As Tapser looked up, he saw the phantom highwayman above him, blunderbuss in hand. And from afar he seemed to hear a voice say,

'Stand and deliver!'

'Hugh Rua,' he gasped sickly to himself.

'Stand and deliver!' he seemed to hear the phantom figure say again.

Tapser's head was spinning. He felt an arm going around him, and a cool breeze in his face as he was carried through the night, holding on for dear life behind the phantom rider. The cape was flapping in his face and he reached up to brush it away but lost his grip and found himself falling, falling, falling . . .'

'Tapser,' he heard a voice saying.

He looked up. Someone was bending over him, and a coat was brushing his face. He pushed it aside and saw the dark figure of the phantom highwayman and his horse rearing up into the night sky.

'Tapser, are you all right? This is Cowlick.'

Slowly Cowlick came into focus. Roisin and Rachel were there too.

'Where am I?' he asked.

'At the memorial,' Rachel told him.

He blinked and looked up at the statue of Hugh Rua and his horse. 'Give me a hand,' he said.

'What happened?' asked Roisin.

'Let's get him down to the house first,' said Cowlick. 'He seems a bit dazed.'

By the time they reached the house, the cool night air had helped Tapser to get over his gulp of poteen. Now and then he felt as if he was going to get sick, but otherwise he had recovered enough to lie on the bed and tell the others what had happened.

'Sorry we were so long in catching up with you,' said Cowlick. 'But I was fast asleep when you woke me. So were the girls.'

'I thought you were close behind me,' said Tapser.

'I didn't know you had gone until I woke up properly,' Cowlick told him.

'And by the time we all got dressed, you must have been up on the High Road,' said Roisin.

'We thought Cowlick was having us on when he told us you had seen the phantom highwayman,' said Rachel. 'Are you sure it wasn't your imagination?'

'The trees up there can look very scarey at night,' said Roisin gently.

'It was him all right,' Tapser asserted. 'And if he hadn't come along when he did, dear knows where I'd be now.'

'Do you think it was the same lorry that we saw at the Castle Spa last night?' asked Cowlick.

'Could be. It looked the same, from what I could see of it.'

'And what about the men?' asked Cowlick. 'Did you recognize any of them?'

Tapser shook his head. 'All I know is that they were after me, and they would have got me too if it hadn't been for Hugh Rua.'

'I think you were imagining things,' said Rachel. 'It must have been the poteen you swallowed.'

'But I heard the men saying, "There he is!" and then they caught me,' said Tapser.

'That was us,' Roisin told him.

'That's right,' said Cowlick. 'We carried you back to the memorial. We didn't see any smugglers — or phantoms.'

'But Hugh Rua saved me from them,' said Tapser. 'I heard him saying, "Stand and deliver."'

'Don't be silly,' said Rachel, 'that must have been Cowlick. He told us to stand aside and give you air.'

Tapser, however, was far from convinced. 'What about the poteen? That wasn't my imagination.'

'You can say that again,' said Cowlick. 'The smell from your breath would knock you down.'

'There you are then,' said Tapser. 'What did I tell you?' He groaned and added, ' I never realized poteen was such horrible stuff. And Mr. Stockman's right. It would drive you round the bend. I'll never drink when I grow up, that's for sure.'

6 THE MOUNTAINY MEN

Because he wasn't feeling well, Tapser didn't have go to church next morning. Instead he slept late, and when he came down for his dinner he found the girls had already changed into their jeans and were waiting for Peppi.

'Here, get that inside you,' said his aunt, 'and you'll feel a lot better. You want to be careful and not be eating too many of them oul' blackberries.'

'Ours would eat them until they were coming out of their ears,' said his uncle. 'But it doesn't seem to do them any harm.'

During-dinner none of them said anything about what they had seen at the Castle Spa or what had happened to Tapser up on the High Road. They still had a lot of finding out to do and, anyway, they had promised Peppi they wouldn't discuss what was going on with anyone else.

True to his word, Peppi arrived shortly after dinnertime,

and they set off for the mountains. He had emptied the caravan, but since it was still going to be a hard pull for the horse he suggested that Tapser and Cowlick should sit on either side of him so that they could jump out and push if the going got too tough. The girls could sit just inside the door, and change places with the boys on the way back down. As for Prince, he seemed content to run alongside.

'Tapser says he saw the phantom highwayman last night,' said Roisin.

'I *did* see him,' said Tapser, and went on to tell Peppi everything that had happened.

'And how do you feel now?' asked Peppi.

'Okay. But the others don't believe me.'

'We didn't say that,' protested Cowlick.

'You didn't have to say it. I could see you didn't. I don't suppose you believe me either, Peppi?'

'I believe there's something very peculiar going on up here. Mind you, I have been keeping a very close eye on the High Road and I haven't seen Hugh Rua. But there are others besides yourself who say they have.'

Cowlick told Peppi what they had seen at the Castle Spa, and wondered if the lorry Tapser had seen could have been going there.

'It could have been all right,' said Peppi. 'But if Max and his men are bringing poteen down by lorry, what are they bringing in by boat?'

'That's what we were wondering,' said Roisin.

'We thought maybe the poteen was being bottled at the Castle Spa and sold to tourists,' said Tapser.

'I wish it was as simple as that,' said Peppi. 'But our men have already checked the shop and their retail sales seem to be in order. They've also been at the harbour keeping a close eye on their exports. They seem to be in order too. Even the ship-load that left yesterday.'

'I don't understand it,' sighed Rachel.

'Don't worry,' Peppi consoled her. 'Neither does anyone else.' He handed the reins to Cowlick and took out his pipe and filled it. 'You know,' he said between puffs, 'you've done very well. You've found out more in one night than I have since I came here. You even found me out. What made you suspicious?'

'Your gloves,' Roisin reminded him.

'Oh aye, so you said.'

'We thought it odd that you should wear them all the time,' explained Rachel.

'Hmmm ... well, you're right you know. When I took up this job as a cover, my hands were soft and white. I knew people who worked with their hands would soon see that I wasn't accustomed to working with mine. So I came up with the idea of wearing these gloves.'

Tapser and Cowlick looked back to see the girls smiling, as if to say, 'We told you so.'

'We also thought Pandora's box might contain a secret,' said Rachel.

'You know, you should be the detectives, not me,' smiled Peppi. 'But I hope you haven't told anybody.'

They all shook their heads and assured him his secret was safe with them.

Then Cowlick thought of something. 'But Peppi ... I mean ... what do we call you now?'

'Just continue to call me Peppi. That suits me fine. If you didn't, other people might become suspicious too.' As they jogged on, he asked, 'What made you suspect that Max van Weshal might be up to something?'

'I thought it was funny that anyone should be exporting

water in the first place,' said Tapser.

'Hmmm, I suppose it might look odd,' said Peppi, 'but it's not so remarkable when you think about it. We take water for granted in this country. But in some countries the water isn't as good as ours, and in some places they've none at all.'

'Do you think Whaler and Scamp could be doing something behind Max's back?' wondered Rachel.'

'I don't think so,' said Peppi. 'They don't do a thing except on Max's say-so.'

'I didn't think it would be worth anyone's while to smuggle poteen,' said Roisin. 'I mean, all I ever heard of was the odd bottle coming down from the mountains at Christmas.'

'That's right,' said Rachel. 'I didn't think the Customs and Excise would be interested in a small thing like that.'

'Ah, but that's the point,' Peppi told them. 'It's not a small thing — not any more. During the past year a lot of it has been finding its way into Europe. And my inquiries have led me to believe it's coming from the general area of this glen. That's why Pandora and Company was formed.'

Cowlick looked puzzled. 'How could our glen be responsible for sending poteen to Europe? I mean, that really would be big business.'

Peppi nodded. 'It is big business, and if it's not stopped soon it could grow into an even bigger business. So you see, it's not just a few bottles for Christmas any more. Judging by the volume of exports, my theory is that someone has set up a big still in the glen or up here in the mountains.'

'You mean their own private distillery?' asked Roisin.

'Exactly.'

'But how could they hide it?' asked Tapser.

'Good question,' said Peppi. 'Unless it's been concealed in a farm or old building, or built underground.'

'Like the bottling plant at the Castle Spa,' said Cowlick. 'It's in a big cavern.'

'I imagine it would have to be something like that,' agreed Peppi. 'But as I say, we've checked the Castle Spa, and that machine is just what Max says it is—a bottling machine.'

'So it must be made up here on the mountain and brought down by lorry,' said Tapser. 'But how does the phantom highwayman come into it?'

'Unless,' suggested Peppi, 'it's some sort of decoy — you know, to draw attention to the High Road when the stuff has reached the Spa.'

'Do you think Max may be behind this phantom business too?' asked Cowlick.

'Well, I think it's more likely to be him and his men than Sam Stephenson or Blind Jack. For a foreigner, Max has taken a great interest in Hugh Rua. He was the one who suggested erecting the memorial to him on the High Road — and what's more, he paid for it.'

'And he sings the *Ballad of Hugh Rua* any chance he gets,' said Roisin.

'But if that's what they're doing,' argued Tapser, 'how do you account for what happened to me? I mean, Hugh Rua appeared when the lorry was still up at the High Road.'

'Exactly,' said Peppi. 'Because it had broken down, so the phantom rider appeared too soon.'

'But he helped me, not them,' Tapser pointed out.

'We were the only ones who helped you as far as I could see,' said Roisin.

'That's right,' said Rachel. 'You must have been drunk.'

The girls giggled, but Tapser just ignored them.

'Whatever about Hugh Rua,' said Cowlick, 'he didn't imagine the lorry, and it was poteen they were smuggling.'

'Precisely,' said Peppi. 'So, assuming it was another delivery for Max, how is he getting the stuff out?' He gave his horse a flick with the reins and puffed on his pipe thoughtfully, before continuing, 'Now, I could understand if he was shipping it out. But you say he was shipping it in. That's the part that puzzles me.'

'Us too,' said Roisin. 'And how did the bottle we found come to be in the sea? That's another mystery.'

'There are a lot of mysteries in this case,' Peppi told them. 'And the biggest one is the source. I mean, the Widow Mulqueen makes a bottle or two. I know that. And so do half a dozen others I know of. But where's the big still? That's what I want to find out. Once we have that, we have the lot.'

They all wished they could help Peppi find the big still, but they couldn't imagine where he might even start looking.

As Peppi's old horse plodded slowly up the mountain road, they passed the Widow Mulqueen's place. It was an isolated farmstead at the end of a long stony lane.

'I wouldn't fancy living up there,' said Tapser.

'It's a bit out of the way all right,' agreed Peppi.

'And there's Max,' said Cowlick. 'He's fixing the Widow's tractor.'

The girls stuck their heads out through the doorway to see. They could just make out Max's white coat as he bent down at the engine. Straightening up, he wiped his hands on a rag and gave them a wave.

'But if Mrs. Mulqueen is making poteen,' said Tapser,

'how come she hasn't been arrested?'

'Well,' Peppi explained, 'it's one thing knowing that she makes the stuff. It's another thing catching her at it. But you never know who we might catch before we go back. Giddyup there.'

They all looked at each other and wondered what Peppi meant, but he told them no more.

Farther up the road, Peppi guided his horse on to a narrow track and after some time pulled in to the side. 'Now,' he said, leading them up to the shadow of a large boulder, 'I want to show you something.'

From the cover of the boulder they scanned the valley below them. There was a lake in the middle of it, and it looked as peaceful and picturesque as a postcard.

'Look,' pointed Peppi. 'Down there ... and there ... and there.'

They followed his directions, and to their surprise saw uniformed men, whom Peppi informed them were police and Excise officers, lying in wait not far from the lake.

'What are they watching?' asked Tapser.

'There's a poteen still down near the edge of the lake,' Peppi explained.

'Do you mean we're watching an actual raid?' asked Roisin.

'With a bit of luck. They know the stuff's there, and they're hoping to catch the men who are making it.'

Time passed, but nothing happened. The waiting officers shifted restlessly. It was obvious they had been there for some time and were feeling cramped.

Peppi's horse scraped the rocky ground with its hoof and threw up its head to get the remaining contents of a nosebag. Prince lay and watched Tapser as he and the others watched the valley.

'There they are,' said Peppi suddenly. 'Keep down.'

'Where?' they whispered.

'Over there to the right . . .'

Peppi's eyes were sharp. It was several minutes before they could see what he had spotted. Three men were making their way towards the still. They wore peaked caps, old tweedy jackets, baggy trousers and wellingtons. Typical mountainy men, they also carried sticks to help them along.

Gradually the men approached the still, unaware that they were walking into a trap. Taking great care not to be seen, the police and Excise men watched and waited. Then, as the three reached the still and began taking off the covering sacks, the two nearest Excise men pounced.

The mountainy men, however, soon showed they weren't to be trifled with. As the other officers of the law made their way down to the lake, the two Excise men found themselves being flailed with the heavy ends of the sticks, which were being wielded like shillelaghs and with the same effect. The two Excise men went down under the blows, and as the policemen drew their batons and clambered over the rocks to lend a hand the mountainy men, far from being trapped at the water's edge, jumped into a small boat which they had hidden in the rushes and rowed furiously out into the lake. The officers stopped at the water's edge, pushed back their caps and stood hands on hips, frustrated and perplexed.

'Why don't they run around and cut them off?' asked Tapser.

'They know they'd never make it,' said Peppi. 'It's a lot longer than it looks from here. It's boggy and by the time they'd get around to the other side they'd be too exhausted to chase them. Anyway, they're not used to the mountain. Those men are. They'd never catch them. Come on. Let's go home.'

'I suppose,' ventured Tapser, 'that isn't the big still you're looking for?'

Peppi laughed. 'I wish it was. But I'm afraid that's only one of the wee stills.'

Roisin and Rachel sat beside Peppi on the way down.

'How well do you know the shore?' he asked them.

Roisin shrugged. 'As well as anybody else I suppose. Why?'

'Because I want you to do something for me. That is, if you still want to help me find the smugglers.'

They assured him they did and, as the boys leaned out through the doorway to hear what he had to say, he went on, 'I think what you saw at the Castle Spa may turn out to be a very important part of this jigsaw. So I want you to try and find the cave that goes in under it.'

'And what will you be doing?' asked Tapser.

'I must find out where the stuff is coming from,' Peppi told them. 'But if you could find the entrance to that cave from the sea-shore, it would be a great help.'

'There are a lot of caves down there,' said Cowlick. 'But I don't think it should be too hard to find.'

'And we were going to look for it anyway,' added Tapser.

'Good,' said Peppi, 'but be careful.'

'And what about our folks?' asked Rachel. 'How much can we tell them?'

'Tell nobody anything,' advised Peppi. 'At least, not yet. Remember what I said. Secrecy is most important at this stage. Whoever's involved in this business, they're in it for big money, and if the news gets out that we're after them it could be very dangerous. So mind yourself.'

7 STOWAWAYS

After tea, Cowlick got the torch and they made their way out to the rocks on the far side of the harbour. It was a lovely evening. Gulls were circling the cliffs and terns were hovering gracefully off-shore before diving for small fish in the incoming tide.

Caves on the sea-shore were something new to Tapser, and he found that they were cold, damp and slippery, not the least like the ones he had read about in books. Somehow he thought they would be dry and warm, like the one Robinson Crusoe had lived in.

'We know every inch of the caves on our own side of the harbour,' Roisin told him as they went from one cave to another, 'but we don't come over here much.'

They were in a fairly big cave now, and Cowlick crouched and shone the torch up into it. 'Another dead end,' he announced.

'But we must be nearly opposite the Castle Spa by

now,' said Rachel.

'Well, that seems to be the last one on this side of the point,' said Cowlick, 'and I think it's time we were getting back.'

'We'll just have to continue the search in the morning,' said Roisin. 'If we can't get around the point we'll try and get down to the rocks on the far side.'

They turned to go.

'Where's Prince?' asked Tapser.

They looked around. The collie was nowhere to be seen, and Tapser called him again and whistled.

'There he is,' said Cowlick. 'Down by the water's edge at the point.'

Prince barked and disappeared again.

'Come on boy,' called Tapser, 'we've got to go.' When Prince didn't come, he made his way over the rocks to see what was keeping him. Moments later he shouted to the others, 'I think he's discovered another cave.'

Cautiously they slithered down the rocks and edged their way around to the point. There they found Prince exploring a large round cave. It was much nearer to the sea than any of the other caves — so much so that the water went in a short distance with each wave, and drained back out.

'I think this is the one we're looking for,' said Roisin.

'Let's tell Peppi,' Rachel suggested.

'We'll have to make sure first,' said Tapser.

'All right, but we must be careful,' warned Cowlick. 'We don't want to be cut off.'

'Oh, I don't know,' said Rachel as they made their way into the cave. 'I don't think Peppi meant us to go into it, just to find it for him.'

'Shush,' said Cowlick, 'and keep together.'

They could see by the light of the torch that the cave was deep.

'I still think we should turn back and tell Peppi,' whispered Rachel.

'Listen,' said Tapser. 'I can hear something. Come on, we can't turn back now.'

Soon they came to a large cavern. Climbing on to a shelf of rock, they saw several tunnels branching off it. One was blocked by an iron gate, and peering through they found themselves looking into the bottling plant at the Castle Spa. White-coated workers were operating the machine, which sparkled and spun as it filled a seemingly endless row of bottles, capped them and placed them into crates.

'There's Max,' whispered Roisin. 'But I don't see Whaler or Scamp.'

'Let's see where these other caves lead to,' said Tapser. 'They might bring us out on top.'

Tapser held on to Prince, and holding on to each other they tip-toed into the nearest tunnel. Here and there Cowlick stopped to shine his torch around the damp walls.

'We seem to be going up all right,' whispered Roisin.

'But where to?' came Rachel's voice from behind.

'That's a good question,' said Cowlick, straining his eyes to peer ahead of them.

'Well, we've come this far,' said Tapser. 'We might as well keep going.'

Eventually even Tapser had to admit that they were getting nowhere. 'Maybe Rachel's right,' he said. 'We'd better go back out the way we came and tell Peppi.'

That, however, was easier said than done. The way back wasn't as easy to find as they thought, and nowhere did the light seem to fall on anything familiar.

'We're lost,' said Cowlick at last.

'No we're not,' said Tapser. 'Not as long as we have Prince.'

'What are you going to do?' asked Roisin.

'Let him scout around. He should be able to pick up the scent we left on the way up.'

'What if he barks?' asked Rachel. 'The men might hear him.'

'That's a chance we'll have to take.'

Tapser released Prince and off the collie went. After sniffing this tunnel and that, he seemed to make up his mind and disappeared down one of them.

'Come on,' whispered Tapser. 'He's found it.'

A short time later they were back at the iron gate. They helped each other down over the shelf of rock and hurried along the cave towards the shore. Less than half way along it, however, they were horrified to find their way blocked by the incoming tide. They were trapped!

Running back, they crouched close together in a tunnel near the iron gate and wondered what they were going to do.

'There's nothing for it but to sit tight,' said Tapser.

It wasn't long before the waves were edging their way into the cavern, and bit by bit the water began to rise until at last it was level with the shelf of rock.

'If the water rises any higher we'll all be drowned,' cried Rachel.

'Don't worry,' said Cowlick gently. 'It won't. We're on the same level as the bottling plant.'

'Listen,' warned Tapser, clamping a hand over Prince's nose to keep him quiet. 'Someone's coming.'

They held their breath. They could hear the iron gate being opened, and saw the white-coated workers stacking crates of bottles on the shelf of rock near the water's edge.

Suddenly bright lights illuminated the cavern, the sound of a boat's engine filled the air, and they saw Whaler and Scamp steer one of Max's lobster boats up to the shelf of rock. Other workers tied ropes to rusty iron rings in the rock, and when the boat was moored tightly Whaler and Scamp removed a canvas cover from a pile of crates.

One by one they lifted the crates and handed them up out of the boat to the other workers who took them into the bottling plant. When this had been done the crates that had been brought out earlier were handed down and stacked in the boat. Whaler and Scamp covered them with the sheet of canvas, climbed out and went into the plant.

'I wonder what they're up to?' asked Cowlick.

'I don't know,' said Tapser, 'but there's something funny going on.'

'I agree,' said Roisin. 'We've got to get out of here somehow and tell Peppi.'

'But how?' asked Rachel.

'Let's try this other tunnel,' said Tapser, 'and see where it leads to.'

Quietly they stole along the other tunnel and to their surprise found it to be quite short. However it offered no way out either, for it sloped down to the bottling plant. To make matters worse, Prince lost his footing on the slippery surface. Cowlick and Rachel stepped forward to catch him and, as Tapser and Roisin looked on horrified, the three of them skidded down the slope and tumbled out on to the floor of the bottling plant!

Chaos followed. Startled workmen grabbed Cowlick and Rachel. Prince made a run for it and was chased by other workmen. Only Max seemed to keep calm. 'There are probably two more of them,' he told Whaler and Scamp. 'The girl and the boy with the red hair. Find them.'

Immediately Tapser and Roisin turned and ran as quickly and as quietly as they could, back the way they had come. Behind them they could hear Whaler and Scamp scrambling up the slippery slope. Pausing at the iron gate, they wondered where to hide. On their left was the tunnel where they had got lost. They weren't going to go in there again.

'Into the boat,' said Tapser. 'Quick'.

Climbing on board, they crawled in under the canvas and lay still just as Whaler and Scamp arrived.

'No one here, boss,' they heard Whaler say.

'Then take out the boat,' ordered Max. 'Quickly, we have no time to lose.'

The engine started and Tapser and Roisin could feel

the boat moving out of the cave. Now and then it scraped against the sides. Then they felt it smashing against the waves, and finally settling down to a steady rise and fall as it reached the open sea.

'I wonder where we're going?' whispered Roisin.

'I don't know,' replied Tapser from the darkness beside her. 'If we could only see out.'

'I think we're at the bow,' said Roisin. 'That means Whaler and Scamp are probably back at the tiller.'

Slowly they eased themselves up round to a sitting position. They parted the canvas cover where it was folded over in front of them. It was dark, and at first they couldn't see a thing. Gradually, as their eyes adjusted to the night, they could make out the stars. The stars rose and fell before them and the noise of the engine was deafening as it pushed the boat farther out to sea.

After a while they began to feel cramped from sitting in the same position for so long. They were also beginning to feel sea-sick when the tone of the engine changed and they started to slow down.

'We're coming to land,' said Tapser. 'I can just make out the cliffs.'

'That's not land,' Roisin told him. 'That's a ship.'

'You're right. I can see it clearer now.'

'It's got its lights switched off. But it looks like a cargo ship.'

'I bet it's the one from the harbour,' said Tapser. 'Remember, Peppi said it left yesterday.'

Before they could say anything more, Whaler shouted 'Ahoy!' and from high in the darkness came an answering call. They were close to the ship now and soon it was looming over them like a solid black wall. There were many voices, foreign voices, and Whaler and Scamp were talking back up to them.

A few minutes later there was the sound of wheels turning aboard the ship, and the clanking of a chain. Under the canvas, Tapser and Roisin heard Scamp scurrying around before climbing on top of the crates and tightening something up around them.

'Oh, no,' whispered Roisin. 'We're being winched on board!'

Above them, unseen eyes watched as the consignment of crates was lifted from the lobster boat, swung in over the ship and lowered into a darkened hold. There was a bump, and the canvas cover went slack. With hearts thumping, Tapser and Roisin waited to be discovered. The minutes ticked by. They could hear voices far above them. Still nothing happened. Cautiously they peeped out.

'It's pitch dark,' whispered Tapser. 'Come on.'

Pulling aside the canvas, they scrambled across the floor

of the hold and hid behind some large wooden boxes.

'I wonder what's happening?' said Roisin.

Even as she spoke the covers of the hold were drawn across and lights were switched on. Men arrived to remove the canvas cover and stack the crates to one side.

'It says spa water,' said Tapser. 'But I bet it's poteen.'

'So that's how they do it,' muttered Roisin. 'The ship leaves the harbour with spa water, and then they swap cargoes!'

'Shuu,' warned Tapser. 'Somebody's coming.'

From their hiding place, they could see Whaler and Scamp, and another man in a peaked cap who looked like the captain, coming down into the hold. They stopped and looked at the crates of poteen, before walking across to a door and into a room that seemed to be full of gauges and clocks and things.

'That must be the engine room,' observed Tapser.

'I'd love to know what they're saying,' said Roisin.

'I think they've some sort of problem,' Tapser told her. 'Look at the way they're pointing at the gauges. And the captain's throwing up his hands as if to say what can he do about it.'

'And look at Whaler,' said Roisin. 'He's worried.'

Whaler took off his cap and wiped the sweat from his brow with the sleeve of his coat.

'I wonder if they're broken down? 'whispered Tapser.

'I hope so,' replied Roisin. 'Or dear knows where we'll end up. I mean, how are we going to get off this thing?'

Before Tapser could answer, the engine started up and the captain, Whaler and Scamp went above deck. A shudder ran through the ship and it started to move. A few minutes later, however, the engine died down again.

'They're having trouble all right,' said Tapser. 'With

a bit of luck they'll have to pull into the nearest port.'

'I hope you're right,'said Roisin.'I don't fancy ending up in some foreign port. How would we get back? And what about our folks? They won't know what has happened to us.'

'Not to mention Cowlick and Rachel. I wonder what's happened to them?'

'Oh, I do hope they're okay. Rachel was right. We shouldn't have gone into that cave in the first place.'

'Well it can't be helped now,' said Tapser.

'But what are we going to do?' asked Roisin. 'Cowlick and Rachel won't know where we've gone. So they can't help us, and we can't help them.'

The same thoughts were going through Tapser's mind, but he didn't want to add to Roisin's worries. Somehow he felt responsible.

'Listen,' cried Roisin. 'They've got the engine going again. We're moving!'

8 TRAPPED IN THE MIST

When Cowlick and Rachel slid down on to the floor of the bottling plant after Prince and were seized by some of the workers, they felt sure Whaler and Scamp would return with Tapser and Roisin. The last thing they expected to hear Whaler saying was that there was no one else there. Where could they have gone in such a short time? Unless they had nipped into the other tunnel. If so, they had fooled Whaler and Scamp. Cowlick and Rachel gave each other a knowing glance. They were both thinking the same. With Tapser and Roisin free, it would only be a matter of time before they raised the alarm. In the meantime, however, they were both prisoners, held firmly by some of Max's men while others tried to catch Prince.

Seeing the collie playing hide-and-seek around the crates and machinery, Max told his men, 'Do not waste your time. He cannot leave here.' Turning to Cowlick and Rachel, he added, 'And neither, I'm afraid, can you, my young friends.'

'What are you going to do with us?' asked Cowlick, hoping his voice didn't sound panicky.

'Do not worry,' said Max, 'I am not going to hurt you. But you will have to be my guests for a while.' Then to the men he said, 'Tie them up.'

'Where will we put them?' asked one of the men.

'This is as good a place as any,' Max told him. 'Take them inside.'

Cowlick and Rachel were taken into an office and bound hand and foot to two chairs.

'At least they didn't gag us the way they do in the films,' said Cowlick.

Rachel managed a forlorn smile, 'Nobody would hear us anyway.'

'That's what they think,' said Cowlick. 'They don't know Tapser and Roisin are somewhere around. So cheer up. We'll be out of here in no time.'

A short time later Max came in. 'I am afraid I must leave you.'

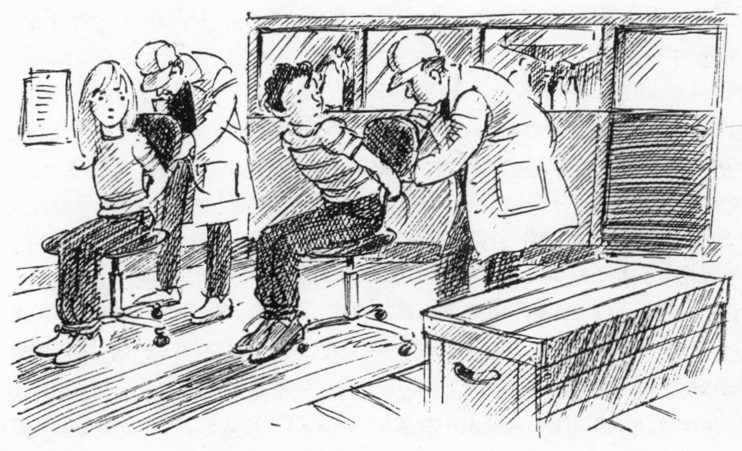

'Where are you going?' asked Cowlick.

'We are finished here now — thanks to you. But we were almost finished anyhow. I am sorry to have to leave you like that, but you have given me no choice.' So saying, and with a slight bow of his head he turned and left.

Somewhere above them, Cowlick and Rachel heard a heavy door banging shut. After that, the only sound to be heard was the lapping of the water beyond the iron gate.

'What are we going to do?' asked Rachel.

'Let's see if we can edge the chairs over to the door.'

As they shuffled their chairs across the floor of the office, Prince pushed open the door and put his front paws up on their lap.

'Good boy, Prince,' said Cowlick. 'Fetch Tapser. Go on, that's a good boy.'

Prince went out and they watched from the doorway as he climbed up the slippery slope of the adjoining tunnel, and reappeared a few moments later at the water's edge beyond the iron gate. He sniffed the ground, looked around uncertainly and returned to them.

'Go on boy, seek'm,' urged Cowlick, and he shouted, 'Tapser, Roisin. We're over here.'

'In the office,' called Rachel.

The only answer they got, however, was the echo of their own voices.

'Where can they have got to?' asked Rachel. There was a tremble in her voice as she put into words her brother's own unspoken question.

'I don't know,' he said, 'but don't worry. No harm can come to us here. We'll just have to try and free ourselves, that's all.'

That, as it turned out, was easier said than done. For

what seemed hours, the two of them twisted and turned and wriggled and pulled, but their bonds remained secure.

'They must be seamen's knots,' gritted Cowlick as he twisted his fingers up around to the knots again. 'The cord's a bit looser but the knots are tighter than ever.'

'Maybe Prince could pull them loose,' suggested Rachel. 'You know, the way they do in the films. Come on, Prince. Here, untie me, that's a good boy.'

'He doesn't understand you.'

'Well, it always works on the telly.'

'Let's back up to each other and see if we can get them loose that way,' said Cowlick.

Rachel sighed. 'All right. I suppose it's worth a try.'

By now, both were cold and tired. Their wrists stung from the constant twisting against the cord. Their fingers ached to the bone and their nails hurt to the very quick from all the pulling and pushing and poking at the knots.

Beyond the iron gate the water had disappeared with the ebbing tide. Morning was approaching.

Prince lay on the floor of the office, watching as Cowlick and Rachel, sitting back-to-back, continued to wrestle with the cords that kept them from escaping and raising the alarm.

'I think you're getting somewhere,' said Cowlick. 'Keep going.'

Rachel pulled and pulled at the cord on her brother's wrist. Her nails were in bits.

'You've done it!' cried Cowlick at last, pulling his hands free. Quickly he untied the cord binding his legs, and set about freeing Rachel.

'Hurry,' she urged him. 'Hurry.'

A moment later Rachel was free too and, pausing only long enough to stretch their cramped arms and legs, they dashed across the floor of the bottling plant, jumped down off the rocky ledge and ran down the cave to the sea. Prince was ahead of them, standing on the rocks barking for all he was worth. Climbing up to where he was, they almost cried with relief at what they saw. Clambering across the rocks to meet them was a search party led by Peppi.

Aboard the cargo ship Tapser and Roisin sat up with a start. It seemed that the engine had been going all night. Now it had stopped, and the clanking of a heavy chain told them that the anchor had been dropped. Climbing a series of steep, metal stairways, they edged along a narrow corridor, and stepping out through an equally narrow doorway, found themselves on deck. So far, so good, they thought, and hurrying across the deck, hid among several large coils of rope.

It was almost dawn and a cold sea mist curled in around the ship. Now and then a flash of light indicated that somewhere nearby a lighthouse was warning shipping of the danger of rocks. For a moment the mist thinned and they caught a glimpse of a dark blob of land.

'Where do you think we are?' asked Tapser.

'I don't know. They must have steamed up the coast.'

The sound of an engine of a smaller boat came to their ears, and two members of the crew dropped a rope ladder over the side. The sound of the engine died away, and a few minutes later the crewmen helped two figures aboard.

'It's Whaler and Scamp!' whispered Roisin. 'We must have been going slowly for them to keep up.'

'So they *must* have engine trouble.'

The captain was there now. Whaler pointed towards

the land and they heard the words, 'Church Bay.'

'Did you hear what they said?' whispered Roisin. 'Church Bay. That means we're off Rathlin Island.'

After further discussion, Whaler and Scamp followed the captain and disappeared from view.

Roisin shivered and pulled her cardigan tightly around herself. 'That sea mist is freezing.'

'Maybe that's our best chance,' said Tapser.

'To do what?'

'To get ashore and raise the alarm. They wouldn't see us in the mist.'

'You mean swim? It's too dangerous. We'd never make it.'

Tapser shrugged. 'I don't know. It just seems so near.'

'It's farther than you think,' Roisin told him. 'And the currents here can be very strong. This is where the Atlantic meets the North Channel. There are whirlpools and everything. Local people call it the Sound, but I once heard a fisherman call it the *Brochan*.'

'The *Brochan*? What does that mean?'

'He was talking to my father, but I think he said it was an Irish word meaning boiling porridge. So you can imagine what it's like.'

Conscious now of the rise and fall of the ship on the swell of the sea, Tapser was quiet as he considered their predicament. 'That means we've no hope then,' he said at last.

'That's what Robert the Bruce thought,' said Roisin.

'Who?'

'Robert the Bruce. He took refuge on Rathlin after his defeat by the English in 1306, and when he was hiding in a cave he watched a spider trying to climb a thread. It wouldn't give up, and he decided he wouldn't give up either. So he went back and fought on and became King of Scotland.'

'I know the story,' said Tapser, 'but I didn't realize it happened on Rathlin.'

Roisin nodded. 'So we'd better put our thinking caps on too.'

'But what can we do? It'll take more than a spider's thread to get us out of this mess.'

'The rope ladder!' exclaimed Roisin. 'It's still hanging over the side. Maybe we can hide in the lobster boat again.'

'That's it, the lobster boat,' said Tapser. 'They'll probably have to put ashore at Rathlin.'

'Or Ballycastle. It doesn't matter where, as long as we get off this ship.'

'Come on so,' urged Tapser. 'Better hurry before they come back.'

Creeping over to the side of the ship, they could just make out the lobster boat lying below them. There was no one around, and without a word they climbed over on to the rope ladder. Gingerly they made their way down.

The ship itself was fairly steady, but not the lobster boat, and Roisin looked down as Tapser stretched out a leg to try and get a foot on board. 'Careful,' she warned. 'Careful.'

The lobster boat rose and fell and rose again. Tapser dropped into it, picked himself up and reached for Roisin. The boat pulled away for a moment, and Roisin held on. A second later it was below her again. 'Now!' said Tapser and pulled her on board.

They found that the canvas cover had been stored back on board, and once more they crawled underneath. After a while, voices and the sharp movement of the boat told them that Whaler and Scamp had followed them down the ladder. The engine burst into life and the boat went racing across the sea.

Under the canvas, Tapser and Roisin waited for the change of sound and movement that would tell them they had arrived at the pier in Church Bay. But the engine continued at the same pitch as the boat churned its way through the sea, and soon it became obvious that Rathlin wasn't to be their destination after all.

'I bet we're going to Ballycastle,' whispered Roisin.

'How far is that?'

'About eight miles.'

'I hope it doesn't take too long. I'm beginning to feel queasy already.'

'Me too,' whispered Roisin. 'But we're going to have to hold on.'

The sea was becoming rougher now. Up and down, up and down, they went, crashing against wave after wave. Grimly they held on, their free hand on their stomach or their mouth. Their stomachs seemed to be moving up and down with each pitch and roll of the boat, and the smell of the diesel and fish added to their nausea. They had an overpowering urge to throw up, but somehow they managed not to. Perhaps it was the fact that they hadn't eaten for so long, or the fear of being discovered. In any event they held on, and after what seemed an eternity the sound of the engine died down.

Cautiously Roisin eased up the edge of the canvas and peeped out. 'The mist is very thick,' she told Tapser. 'I think maybe they've lost their bearings.'

As the boat bobbed about, they waited to see what Whaler and Scamp were going to do. They could hear the two of them talking, probably wondering where they were. The noise of the engine increased slightly and the boat eased its way forward. Somewhere beyond them they could now hear waves breaking on the shore, and suddenly they felt themselves being carried along. A few minutes later the boat scraped aground, and they heard Whaler and Scamp getting out.

Pulling back the canvas, they gulped in mouthfuls of fresh air. They could see that the mist was blowing in low over the sea and had already enveloped Whaler and Scamp. Hardly able to believe their good fortune, they jumped out and ran across the stony beach. Finding their way blocked by the sea wall, they searched around frantically until they found a way up. If only they could get over the top unseen, they knew they just might get away.

However, a sudden roar from Whaler brought them to a halt. Turning around, they saw that a gap in the mist had revealed their presence on the wall.

'That's torn it,' gasped Tapser. 'Hurry.'

Dashing across a narrow road, they climbed over a low ditch and scrambled up a steep grassy slope. Behind them they could hear Whaler and Scamp close on their heels. Fortunately Whaler wasn't built for climbing steep slopes. A wet patch gave way under his enormous weight, and he went sliding back to the bottom. Scamp, anxious as always to please him, made his way down to help. Panting for breath, Tapser and Roisin reached the top and raced across the fields for dear life.

'Where do you think we are?' asked Tapser. The mist had closed in about them again, and knowing they couldn't be seen they had slowed down to get their breath.

'Well, if they were heading for Ballycastle, we're probably somewhere along the coast from it.'

Stumbling into a small sand-pit, they looked back. There was no sign of Whaler and Scamp, and they walked on across the grass.

'I hope Rachel and Cowlick are all right,' said Roisin.

'So do I,' said Tapser. 'If only we could get to a 'phone and raise the alarm. Come on, there must be a house around here somewhere.'

If there was, the mist kept it from their view, but a short time later they came to a road. It was still very early in the morning and there was no sign of any traffic, so they set off down the hill. They came to several houses, and knocked urgently on the doors. There was no reply, and afraid to delay too long they continued on down the road in the hope that it would take them into Ballycastle.

They were wondering where Whaler and Scamp had got to when they came to a car parked in off the road. It seemed to have broken down and a man was working at the engine. Delighted to have found help at last, they ran over to him.

'Thank goodness,' panted Roisin. 'We thought we'd never find anyone. The smugglers. They're after us . You must help us to raise the alarm.'

Lifting his head from the engine, the man suddenly turned and grabbed Roisin by the wrist. 'Now why should I help you to raise the alarm?' he sneered.

'Whaler!' cried Tapser.

Having followed the narrow road up from the sea-front to where it joined the main road, Whaler and Scamp had got ahead of them and were now in the act of stealing a car.

Startled, Roisin struggled to free herself.

'Leave her alone,' shouted Tapser. Rushing forward, he pounded Whaler with his fists, but the big man just laughed and caught him by the scruff of the neck.

In desperation, Tapser kicked out. One of his kicks connected. With a howl of pain Whaler released them and grabbed his shin. Out of the corner of his eye, Tapser could see Scamp getting out from behind the steering wheel.

'Run, Roisin,' he shouted. 'Run.'

A few minutes later they flung themselves behind a ditch and listened for sounds of pursuit. There were none, and Tapser raised his head and looked back.

'Oh, no!' he groaned.

'What is it?' asked Roisin, easing herself up.

'Look,' he whispered, pointing to a spot where the road rose above the mist. 'Coming over the hill.'

Roisin could hardly believe her eyes. From the swirling mist a coach, drawn by four white horses, had emerged. It was gliding down the road towards them, and it was plain to see that even the driver, who sat hunched over the reins, was a ghostly white.

'The phantom highwayman!' she gasped.

9 THE SPIDER'S WEB

Fearing that the phantom highwayman and the poteen smugglers would soon be upon them, Tapser and Roisin ran away from the road and climbed over a stone wall.

'Oh, no,' cried Roisin, finding themselves among headstones. 'We're in a cemetery. This is like a nightmare.'

Beyond the graveyard, they came to the ruins of an old church and took refuge behind its walls. Wreaths of mist were still swirling up from the sea and now, as they looked back, they caught another glimpse of the ghostly coach passing down the road. Again, it was only a fleeting glimpse, a shadow, for it quickly merged with the mist and disappeared.

Roisin shivered, but it wasn't the wet or the cold or even the thought of being in an old church that sent the shiver through her. It was the thought of the phantom coach. 'What can it be?' she wondered. 'I mean what's it doing here? We're miles from the High Road.'

Tapser frowned. 'I don't know, but if somebody's trying to frighten us, they're going the right way about it.'

'What are we going to do?'

'Get to the police and raise the alarm. For all we know Cowlick and Rachel are still prisoners at the Castle Spa.'

'Well, I'm not going out on the road again. Wild horses couldn't drag me.' Roisin paused as she thought of her unfortunate choice of words. 'Anyway, Whaler and Scamp will be out there looking for us when they get that car going.'

'You're right,' said Tapser. 'If they get their hands on us again we're finished. We'll just have to wait here until the mist clears, then go for help.'

A lark sang as it fluttered up to meet the sun. Tapser and Roisin scrambled to their feet and ran outside. They found that the mist had cleared and morning had brought blue sky and sunshine. It had also brought a flow of traffic along the road. They could now see they were on the outskirts of Ballycastle, and realized the reason why they hadn't come across any houses in their flight across the fields was that they had been on the golf links.

Crossing the road, they ran up the neatly cut grass and looked out towards Rathlin. The cargo ship was still anchored at Church Bay.

'Hurry,' urged Roisin. 'We've got to get into Ballycastle and raise the alarm before it gets under way again.'

'What's going on?' wondered Tapser. 'I've never seen so much traffic.'

The vehicles were bumper to bumper now and had slowed to a crawl. As they ran past a lorry loaded with sheep, Roisin said, 'There must be a fair on.' She stopped and grabbed Tapser's arm. 'Of course, it's the Lammas

Fair. Why didn't I think of it before. Come on. There are bound to be people we know. They'll help us.'

Crossing the Margy Bridge, they saw a signpost which told them they had been hiding in the ruins of Bonamargy Franciscan Friary, burial place of the famous chieftain, Sorley Boy Macdonnell. Keeping a sharp lookout for Whaler and Scamp, they hurried along the sea-front, and with another anxious glance towards Rathlin, turned up Quay Road.

There they found that numerous stalls had been erected and traders were selling portable radios, tape recorders, watches and all kinds of nick-nacks.

Suddenly they heard a voice from the other side of the road shouting; 'You're all going to die!'

Startled, they looked around to see a man in black standing on a corner. A placard hanging from his neck bore the Biblical text, 'Prepare to meet thy doom.'

'You're all going to die!' he declared to all and sundry.

Relieved that he wasn't one of their pursuers, but a man proclaiming the word of God, they exchanged a half-hearted smile and hurried on.

The town was bustling with activity, but there was still no sign of the two smugglers — or a policeman. The Diamond, which forms the town centre, was crowded. Stall-holders were shouting about all the bargains they had to offer, and there were cries of 'Dulse and yellow man', as they offered bags of edible sea-weed and lumps of their famous yellow toffee for sale. Everywhere, people were listening, looking, buying or just ambling around.

'There's a policeman,' said Tapser. 'Two of them — over there.'

Before they could reach them, they found their way barred by Whaler and Scamp. Terrified, they turned and ran. Determined not to lise them this time, Whaler and Scamp lunged through the crowd, scattering people in all directions.

Nipping in here, darting through there, Tapser and Roison found themselves pushing and shoving in their anxiety to escape.

'Now hold on there,' said a familiar voice. 'What's all the rush about?'

Looking up they saw to their surprise and great relief that it was none other than Mr. Stockman.

'What are you doing here?' asked Tapser.

'Didn't I tell you I was coming to the Lammas Fair? Now what's your hurry? You'd think somebody was after you.'

'There is,' cried Tapser. 'A phantom coach and...'

'A phantom coach?' smiled Mr. Stockman. 'Sure the only coach I saw was the *Londonderry Mail.* Sam Stephenson's after bringing it over to show it off here at the Lammas Fair.'

Roisin and Tapser looked at each other. The sea mist, they realized, had played tricks with them and given Sam and his coach that ghostly appearance.

'But the smugglers,' insisted Roisin, throwing an anxious glance over her shoulder. 'They're after us. Two of them. Look, that's them there.'

Seeing they were with an adult, Whaler and Scamp had stopped. There was a threatening scowl on their faces and their hands lingered close to their knives.

Mr. Stockman didn't like the look of the two seamen at all and, taking Tapser and Roisin by the hand, began edging through the crowd. Whaler and Scamp followed. So intent were they in doing so, however, that they failed to notice several policemen making their way through the crowd behind them.

Mr. Stockman stopped. Suddenly Tapser found Prince beside him, and as he hugged him he spotted Peppi among the police.

'And there's Rachel and Cowlick,' cried Roisin, jumping up and down with delight.

Realizing now that the tables had been turned, Whaler and Scamp charged through the crowds in a desperate attempt to escape. In doing so they scattered a group of farmers who were admiring a pair of beautiful piebald donkeys. The farmers weren't amused at the intrusion and made to grab them. Whaler swung around to ward them off and collided with the donkeys. To add to the confusion Prince was now barking and snapping at Whaler's feet.

Frightened, one of the donkeys bared its teeth and brayed vigorously. At the same time it swished its tail and lashed out with its hind legs. Both hooves caught Whaler squarely on the seat of his big baggy pants and catapulted him into the arms of the police. Both Whaler and Scamp were promptly relieved of their knives and escorted to the police station, while Tapser and Roisin had a joyful reunion with Cowlick and Rachel, their parents and Peppi.

The Lammas Fair was in full swing, and down on the seafront the *Londonderry Mail* was proving to be a big attraction for those who wanted a break from the hustle and bustle of the Diamond. Mr. Stephenson was up top, and inside were Peppi, Mr. Stockman, Tapser and his cousins, and, of course, Prince. The ride was Mr. Stephenson's way of saying thanks to them all for helping expose the real smugglers and taking suspicion from him.

'And who's this fella Max-what's-his name?' asked Mr. Stockman as he passed around bags of yellow man.

'He's the only one who can answer that,' said Peppi. 'And we have to find him first. The last we heard of him he was heading towards Ballycastle. That's why we came here.'

'Why do you think he came here?' asked Tapser.

'Could be he was trying to link up with Whaler and Scamp. Maybe even the cargo ship.'

'But why were they swapping cargoes?' asked Rachel. 'That's what I don't understand.'

'It's very simple really,' explained Peppi. 'That way the ship ended up with a cargo of poteen and Customs papers to say it was spa water.'

'Well, you've got the ship,' said Cowlick, 'but what about the big still? You didn't find that.'

'But we did,' announced Peppi. 'The papers we found at the plant show that Max had organized supplies from all the people who were making poteen as a small business. Grouping them together, he made it into one big business. And mending machinery was only a cover for keeping in touch with them. So the big still was all around us

— the wee stills of the glen and the mountain. It was staring us in the face and we couldn't see it.'

'A sort of co-op,' suggested Mr. Stockman.

'Or spider's web,' said Roisin, thinking of Rathlin.

'Exactly,' laughed Peppi. 'He had it organized just like a spider's web. But unlike the spider, he had to give up, thanks to yourselves.'

'Was your theory right then?' asked Rachel. 'That the phantom highwayman was something they were doing to take attention away from the smuggling?'

'I think it must have been,' said Peppi. 'But, oddly enough, none of them admit knowing anything about the phantom of Hugh Rua.'

'There you are,' said Tapser. 'What did I tell you? I think the ballad is right. His spirit does still ride in the glen.'

Mr. Stockman smiled. 'Well, don't forget what I told you. The glen has a lot of secrets, and so have its people.'

He winked at Peppi, and Peppi added, 'That's right. I mean, who's to say who was haunting the High Road? Sure if it comes to that, who's to say it's Mr. Stephenson up on top now, and not Hugh Rua?'

Tapser smiled. He knew Peppi was only joking. But even if he wasn't and Hugh Rua had stolen another coach-and-four, he was certain they had nothing to worry about. After all, he had ridden with the phantom highwayman before! Anyway, there were much more pleasant things to think about now than phantoms and smugglers. There was a song in the air, and he knew there were the amusements and many other treats in store for them at what the song called 'the Ould Lammas Fair in Ballycastle O.'

ACKNOWLEDGEMENTS

In my research into stage coaches, highwaymen and various other matters for this story, a number of people and publications have been of great help to me.

Some years ago, when I was looking for details of the Londonderry mail coaches, Mr. J. W. Vitty of the Linenhall Library in Belfast was good enough to delve into his records and provide me with the information I required.

For more general information, I have relied on an article called, 'The Age of the Stage Coach' by Professor J.L. McCracken in *Travel and Transport in Ireland*, edited by Kevin B. Nowlan (Gill and Macmillan, 1973).

I have also drawn from *Old Ballymena*, a history of the town during the 1798 Rebellion, published in the local *Observer* newspaper in 1857 under the title of 'Walks About Ballymena' and reprinted more recently in booklet form.

Rena Dardis of The Children's Press gave me a copy of *The Highwayman in Irish History*, by Terence O'Hanlon (M.H. Gill and Son, 1932) and I found that very useful. I would also like to thank John Lafferty of Derry for telling me about the outlaw, Sean Crosagh Mullan, and for the assistance and encouragement he has given me over the years.

The first poem quoted in this book is *The Death Coach* by T. Crofton Croker, who was born in Cork in 1798. James Lyons has included it in his book, *Legends of Cork*

(Anvil Books, 1988), and I feel James should be commended for his work in tracking down and preserving some of these old legends.

The second poem quoted by Mr. Stephenson, about the vanishing lake of Loughareema, is *The Fairy Lough* by Moira O'Neill. In this connection I would like to thank Jack McCann and Cahal Dallat of the Glens of Antrim Historical Society. When in 1990 I attended the John Hewitt International Summer School in Carnlough, I was privileged to hear a lecture by Cahal Dallat, in which he referred to the fate that befell Col. McNeill and his coachman at Loughareema, which he translated as *Loch an Rith Amach*, the running-out lough.

As far as poteen and poteen-making are concerned, I heard many a story from the late Tim Kelly, of Luggacurren in Co. Laois. Needless to say, some of those stories are reflected in the *Highwayman*, and I am grateful to him and his wife, Kathleen.

ALSO BY TOM McCAUGHREN

The Peacemakers of Niemba
(The Richview Press, 1966).

From The Children's Press
The Legend of the Golden Key (1989; abridged edition 1983)
The Legend of the Phantom Highwayman (1983)
The Legend of the Corrib King (1984)
The Children of the Forge (1985)
The Silent Sea (1987)

From Anvil Books
Rainbows of the Moon (1989)
Short-listed for Irish Book Awards 1990
French translation in preparation by Hachette Jeunesse

From Wolfhound Press
Run with the Wind (1983);
RAI Children's Book Award (1985)
Run to Earth (1984)
Run Swift, Run Free (1986)
Irish Book Award 1987
International Youth Library choice
For WHITE RAVENS 1988
This trilogy also won the Irish Children's Book Trust Bisto Book of the Decade Award (1980-1990), and has been translated into a number of languages.